A SINISTER STRANGER

A tough-looking bozo dressed halfway cowboy and halfway preacher stepped away from the wall to growl, "Might you be that newspaper boy, MacKail, little darling?"

Stringer considered whether to answer before or after he went for his six-gun. Then he decided any man who'd call another man little darling, knowing he was packing a gun of his own, had to be at least as dumb as he might be dangerous, so he answered, "You can call me anything but late for breakfast, *sweetheart*. What's it to you?"

Stringer was braced for most any move but the next one . . .

Also in the STRINGER *series from Charter*

STRINGER
STRINGER ON DEAD MAN'S RANGE
STRINGER ON THE ASSASSINS' TRAIL
STRINGER AND THE HANGMAN'S RODEO
STRINGER AND THE WILD BUNCH
STRINGER AND THE HANGING JUDGE
STRINGER IN TOMBSTONE
STRINGER AND THE DEADLY FLOOD
STRINGER AND THE LOST TRIBE
STRINGER AND THE OIL WELL INDIANS
STRINGER AND THE BORDER WAR
STRINGER ON THE MOJAVE

LOU CAMERON

STRINGER

ON PIKES PEAK

CHARTER BOOKS, NEW YORK

STRINGER ON PIKES PEAK

A Charter Book/published by arrangement with the author

PRINTING HISTORY
Charter Original/August 1989

ISBN: 1-55773-231-0

Charter Books are published by The Berkley Publishing Group,
200 Madison Avenue, New York, New York 10016.
The name "Charter" and the "C" logo are trademarks belonging
to Charter Communications Inc.

PRINTED IN THE UNITED STATES OF AMERICA

10 9 8 7 6 5 4 3 2 1

CHAPTER ONE

The troops bound for Cripple Creek had to change from broad to narrow-gauge rolling stock at Colorado Springs. Hence the scene in the busy Denver & Rio Grande switchyards might have been confusing enough if the sun hadn't been going down, a thunderstorm hadn't been brewing up, and a corporal's squad of the Colorado National Guard hadn't been marching Stringer MacKail across the tangle of tracks at bayonet point.

As they approached the last toylike car of the narrow-gauge combination Stringer had been heading for to begin with, a rear door slid open and a portly part-time officer in khaki pants and an army blue summer shirt popped out onto the observation platform to observe whatever in thunder his corporal of the guard had stumbled over this time.

It appeared at first glance to be a tall tanned cowhand wearing a battered gray Stetson crushed Rough Rider style and separated from his scuffed spurred Justins by a clean and well-fitting but mighty sun-faded outfit of denim jacket and matching jeans.

One of the guardsmen had naturally relieved the mysterious civilian of his sidearm as well as other baggage. But their senior officer could see the gun rig strapped about the prisoner's lean hips rode neither greenhorn high nor gunslinger-on-the-prod low. So he simply growled, "I give up. Are you another gunhand hired by the rough and ready M.O.A. or another union thug sent for by the wild and woolly W.F.M.? In neither case will you be drifting one mile closer to the fun and games up around Cripple Creek, if you know what's good for you!"

The target of his possibly well-meant warning laughed incredulously and replied, "No offense, ah, Major, but this is commencing to get sort of silly. To begin with I've come in peace to cover the big miner's strike for the *San Francisco Sun*. I ride for them as a freelance feature writer and I answer to Stringer MacKail, even if they do have me down as Stuart K. MacKail on my press credentials."

Then he added, "I'd be proud to show you my credentials, if you'd tell these chocolate soldiers not to jab at me with those nickel-plated pig stickers on their infernal Krags."

The paunchy field grade officer stared down even more disgusted to grumble, "Jesus H. Christ, they warned us you and other sob sisters might be coming to put more bad things about us in the outside newspapers. I've read your socialist trash in the papers, MacKail. So I'll take your word you're who you say you are. I can't see any self-respecting gunfighter trying to pass his fool self off as a red flag newspaper boy!"

Stringer frowned hard as he tried to digest that crap about red flags. He couldn't. So he tried, "I think you must have me and my paper mixed up with others, Major. The owners of the *Sun* are hard-shell capitalists and my feature editor, Sam Barca, is inclined to view your average reservation jump as a Marxist plot."

The portly part-time warrior replied in a tone of unimpressed dismissal, "Be that as it may, we have our orders. Neither Governor Peabody nor General Bell want any press coverage during the present, ah, emergency."

Up the line, the small Shay engine tooted its tin whistle and commenced to ring its cow-bell. So the major told his men to hand back Stringer's baggage and sidearm. As Stringer took them with a curt nod of thanks the older man added, not unkindly, "General Bell and his G.H.Q. staff will be staying at the Broadmoor Hotel, here in town. I'm sure our public relations office will be handing out the usual press releases from time to time."

Stringer knew that was a raindrop he'd just felt hitting his hat brim. It still felt as if he was getting spit on. He shook his head and insisted, "You can't do this, Major. The freedom of the press is guaranteed under the Constitution of these United States and, last time I looked, Colorado was one of the same, right?"

The major shrugged again and answered, with a grim little smile, "Feel free to write your congressman, your *own* congressman, California boy. Nobody here said you weren't free as any other bird to flap your sweet way over to the gold fields in the foothills. It just so happens, however, that as of now this railroad, the wagon trace, and every goddamned bridge or tunnel leading in or out of Cripple Creek has been or soon will be sealed off by military personnel, with orders to shoot to kill until further notice!"

Stringer had made his way clear of the switchyards but he was still on railroad property when a mighty whiplash of blinding white lightning disemboweled the dark overcast above. So it was coming down fire and salt by the time he'd made it to the dubious shelter of a deserted baggage platform.

He figured he was already as wet as he needed to be and hunkered down to haul a canary yellow rain slicker from his battered but thoughtfully packed gladstone. Made in Connecticut for the New England fishing trade, the brand was as popular among hands who faced weather as wet on open range or open sea.

Packing his gladstone in his left hand, Stringer sloshed on over towards Nevada Street through the blinding gully washer. He'd waded perhaps twenty yards before he noticed his right hand seemed to be roosting wetly on the hard rubber grips of his double-action S&W .38 by way of the innocent-looking pocket slit on that side of his old slicker. He'd cut away the original cloth pocket a spell back, after barely living through another rainy night with his infernal side arm hung up under all that stiff yellow oilcloth.

But he saw nothing in the swirling darkness all around him to justify such instinctive caution on his own part. He hadn't taken that shoot-to-kill bullshit from a puffed-up, part-time, man-of-destiny too seriously. The pompous fart had talked too big for a man packing a serious punch and, what the hell, nobody had said anything about Downtown Colorado Springs being off limits to the Fourth Estate.

Since they'd refused him a ride on their shitty troop train he knew he was stuck here in more civilized parts for at least the night. Then he suddenly saw why he'd been feeling spooked, and it didn't make him feel one iota better. For anyone could see the evening was young and that he had to be somewhere near the center of town. So why was it black as a bitch betwixt lightning flashes and why were all the windows staring at him as dark as the eye sockets of skulls when the sky above *did* flicker some?

The silvery veils of slashing rain explained why anyone with a lick of sense and a place to be was indoors off the streets right now. But even most cow towns had been wired for electric street lighting by the turn of the century, and Colorado Springs was a cut or more above your average cow town.

It was the county seat as well as being a college town that took some pride in being more up to date than the older Denver to the north or brawling Pueblo to the south and, last time Stringer had looked, both downtown Denver and Pueblo's main street had blazed pretty good this early in the evening, rain or shine.

He was still pondering on why all the lights were out when he spied the cheerful glow of lamplight shining out a batwinged doorway on the far side of the flooded cross street he'd come to. As he stepped off the high sandstone curb into quite an ankle-deep current, he decided Fountain Creek, the normally inches deep trickle running through town had to be well above its usual banks. That inspired Stringer to recall the legendary Cherry Creek Flood they still talked about up in Denver. But as he made it to the far side without being swept out across the prairie to his doom he discovered he was only soaked from the knees down. He knew he'd never get his Justins back on if he let them dry out without his feet inside 'em, so he ignored the way his socks squished inside the soaked leather as he pushed his way through the bat wings to wet his innards with something less disgusting than tepid rainwater off his hat-brim.

It wasn't easy, the welcoming warm glow in a dank sea of darkness had attracted quite a crowd and there were even soggy working girls of the more ladylike persuasion jostling for standing room in the tiny drinking establishment. As Stringer tried to slide the wet back of his slicker along the plate glass saloon front to one end of the bar a half-drowned Gibson Girl told him not to get fresh and went right on blocking his way. He sighed and eased back the other way, about ready to give it all back to the earlier birds, when he heard a familiar voice calling out to him from somewhere in the depths of the jam-packed joint and, knowing he could do it if he really put his back into it, Stringer began to bull his way back to join his fellow Californian and sometimes-friendly rival, Jack London.

The erstwhile oyster pirate and waterfront thug of Frisco Bay had commenced to dress more like a riverboat gambler since he'd sold his big dog story, "Call Of The Wild" to a public Stringer suspected of knowing even less about the recent events in Alaska. But he still needed a good dentist and, even with his mouth shut, always reminded Stringer of a superannuated Irish choirboy with an unwholesome interest in the poor box. As Stringer got within reach, London grabbed him by one arm and muttered, "Back room, if we can get there. I know the boyos here of old. So for God's sake let me do the talking for the both of us and leave off your Adam Smith views on the economy of this great wicked world!"

Stringer didn't argue. Arguing with Jack London on almost any subject was a waste of time. For, like many self-educated men with a greater gift of gab than serious study, the former Marxist and more recent Social Darwinist could argue both sides and often did. Stringer knew that back in '93 a younger Jack London had marched on Washington in the van of Coxey's Red Army and been arrested for walking on the grass in front of the White House. Of course, that had been before old Jack had taken to glorifying the rugged individualists of the Northwest in his blood and thunder novels, and often just as made-up newspaper articles. Stringer could hardly wait to see how old Jack meant to cover the current unrest up near Cripple Creek. For both the crusty Mine Owners Association, and the radical Big Bill Heywood leading the Western Federation Of Miners seemed cut from the whole cloth of a Jack London adventure novel, with either as fit to play the hero or villain, depending on old Jack's current stock portfolio.

It was at times like these that Stringer felt beset about having grown up neither mind-twisting poor nor smug-snob rich. He took pride in reporting things the way they really were and he already knew there were at least three sides to the showdown building to a climax over in the gold fields. There was the Mine Owners' Side, the Mine Workers' Side, and, as always, the *truth*.

Stringer began to suspect he knew which side Jack London would come out for when they found themselves in a back room a third as large but a hell of a lot less crowded than the Black Hole of Calcutta they'd just escaped. His friendly rival was greeted like an old chum by more than one gent seated around the beer schooners and poker chips on a massive round table, and most of them were dressed more like mining men than Stringer was. As Stringer peeled off his wet yellow slicker London announced in a jovial tone, "This cuss ain't really the Sundance Kid, boys. He just led a misspent youth on a cow spread east of Frisco when I was learning to steal oysters. I want you all to meet the one and original Stringer MacKail from the *San Francisco Sun*."

As Stringer hung his slicker on a wall hook, among others of less bright coloration, the big burly cuss dealing the cards at the moment growled, "No more *names*, first or last, if you don't mind, Jack. If you say he's with you, he's welcome back here as an orphan of the storm and no more. For I have read the *San Francisco Sun* and to tell the truth I wouldn't wipe my ass on a rag that would back our darling Teddy Roosevelt for dog catcher."

There was a growl of agreement from the other roughly dressed and somewhat soggy sorts. Jack London led Stringer around to the far side and banged imperiously on what seemed to be the door of a dumbwaiter built into the wall. But when the panel slid open Stringer saw it was just a means of communication betwixt the back room and the crowded bar out front. Jack London told the harrassed-looking barkeep they needed a pitcher of beer back here. It only took a few moments. Once they had it, London led Stringer to a smaller table in one corner, saying, "This'll have to do. Nobody but a Paddy fresh off the boat from Kerry would want to risk a match stem in that game of stud with Big Bill dealing."

Stringer tried not to stare in an obvious manner as he helped himself to a better look at the object of London's dubious flattery. The fact that Big Bill Heywood was a ruggedly handsome giant of around thirty-five was less surprising than the fact he was down here in Colorado Springs at a time the Colorado Guard was fixing to do something serious about him up in Cripple Creek. Stringer wondered if the union organizer knew they were blocking off all the ways in and out, with orders to shoot to kill. He wondered how he was supposed to mention this to a man who'd just said he didn't want to be addressed by his proper name. He wondered what business it was of his own in any case.

Stringer had eaten a late lunch that afternoon while waiting for the Colorado National Guard to show up, for all the good it had done him, but he still hadn't had any supper. So after a polite sip of the beer London poured for both of them, he leaned back and got out the makings, murmuring, "I'd best take it easy on the suds until I figure out where I'll be having a late supper and laying my weary head, tonight, Jack. I don't suppose you'd know a decent hotel within wading distance of this meager shelter?"

London reached expansively inside his frock coat to haul out a hotel key on a polished wooden tab, saying, "You can use up my hired single with bath at the Alta Vista, pard. For I'm just waiting out a midnight special to Cheyenne and, what the hell, I may as well stay here warm and dry as well as closer to the depot."

Stringer was no fool, so he pocketed the key fast, but felt it only fair to ask, "What do I owe you for such hospitality, Jack? I can always charge room and board in the field to my paper and . . ."

"Not the Alta Vista," London cut in, cheerfully. Then, as Stringer looked blank, the more prosperous writer explained, "It's about as ritsy titsy as the Broadmoor over on the far side of the raging flood or, hell, the Brown Palace in Denver or the Saint Francis back home. I paid in advance, figuring on being here over the damned weekend. They don't give refunds, the capitalistic bastards, so why should some fancy dude get to sleep in a fancy layout I've been stuck with?"

Stringer didn't answer as he finished rolling his Bull Durham cigarette. He was a mite annoyed by London's gesture, now that he saw how the joke was supposed to work. But he wasn't annoyed enough to turn down a free hotel room in a crowded town. So he sealed the straw paper carefully with the tip of his tongue and lit the results before he asked, quietly, "Aren't you here to cover the troubles over in Cripple Creek, Jack?"

London shook his head and replied, "There's just not much of a market for appeals to social justice, these days, Stringer. Karl Marx has been dead over twenty years and I fear we've about mined him out. That young Lime-juice writer, H.G. Wells, has been getting off a lot of neat digs at the bloated capitalists with his futuristic novels. You've read his stuff, of course?"

Stringer nodded and said, "I didn't know *The War of the Worlds* was a socialist tract. Which one of his stories are you planning on swiping, Jack?"

London smiled as brazenly as any man with such rotten stumps could smile and answered, "I told you that exclusive you filed on Soapy Smith that time was Public Domain, damn it. Did you really think a true story everyone in Alaska knew about was your own damned private property?"

Before Stringer could answer the back room was

suddenly as brightly lit as broad daylight and almost everyone but Stringer cheered. He just stared up slack-jawed at the overhead Edison bulbs he'd never noticed up there in the smoke filled gloom before. Like most folk of his generation, he'd grown up mostly by gas or coal oil light and tended not to think about electricity as long as things were working halfway reasonable, the way they always had.

Jack London said, "*That's* what I was doing here in Colorado Springs. That's what I thought I was doing, I mean. I was passing through Cheyenne a few days ago when I heard they were having trouble with the electric juice down here, again."

The lights winked off again, plunging them all back into the now much gloomier glow of the one overhead oil lamp. "I'd say they still were," Stringer observed dryly, adding, "What did you mean by *again*?"

London shot him a look of sincere surprise and asked, "Are you saying you never covered that story? It was the wonder of the West and I thought Sam Barca liked to assign such shit to you, pard."

Stringer asked which wonder of the West they were talking about, and when it might have taken place in or near Colorado Springs. When London told him 1899, Stringer nodded thoughtfully and said, "Alaska. I don't see why my paper thought a lad who'd put himself through Stanford punching cows would know beans about panning for gold in ice water, but that's life. What did I miss down *here*?"

London chuckled and said, "I had to read about it later, being as much an old sourdough as you. But, in sum, a mad scientist playing with Rocky Mountain lightning on a night much like this, blew every fuse in Colorado Springs and set the generating plant on fire!"

Stringer frowned, thoughtfully blew some smoke, and decided, "I think I read about it a month or more late in the papers from The States. I'd forgotten Professor Tesla was experimenting with the lightning around Pikes Peak. But we *are* talking about old Nikola Tesla, the Balkan pal of Mark Twain and sworn enemy of Thomas Alva Edison, aren't we?"

London grimaced and replied, "A lunatic by any name would still be spooky. Mark Twain's amusing pal scared the liver and lights out of everyone for miles around with his electricated experiments just west of town. They say he set off private thunderbolts they could hear in Cripple Creek, twenty miles or more up in the Front Range. As if that wasn't satanic enough, they say he gave private showings in his fancy laboratory, juggling ball lightning with his bare hands!"

Stringer shrugged and said, "I wish I'd been there. But what have Tesla's electrical experiments got to do with the pending showdown between the M.O.A. and W.F.M., Jack?"

London shot an uneasy glance at the card game in progress just about at easy earshot and murmured, "Keep it down to a roar. This isn't an official union meeting and in any case, I told you I'm not here as a reporter. I doubt anyone covering the current dispute is going to reap any headlines, and I'm getting too old to duck flocks of migrating bricks. I told you I detoured down this way when I heard they were having more excitement with their electricity in Colorado Springs. I thought old Nick Tesla might have come back to play with the notorious local lightning."

He saw Stringer was having trouble following his full meaning and added, "I have this notion for a futuristic novel about an ideal society run entirely on clean electric current and the eight hour day. Only, to tell the truth, I'm sort of fuzzy as to just how they *make* the juice, or why it makes lamps light and motors run once it gets there. I know Professor Tesla backed the winning side in that big argument about Acey-Ducey between Edison and old George Westinghouse. So I figured as long as I was passing through, and Tesla seems to be so fond of publicity . . ."

"Gotcha." Stringer cut in with a sardonic grin, adding, "I'm sure you meant to cut him in on the profits after mining his brain for your story. Who's plot will you be using, Edward Bellamy's? No offense, but so far it sounds a heap like Bellamy's "Looking Backward" and, correct me if I'm wrong, but doesn't Ed's copyright have a few more years to run?"

London just smiled, not even sheepishly. One of the reasons he and Stringer got along so well was that it only annoyed London to be called a plagiarist when a critic added that the idea he'd stolen was *boring*. He told Stringer in a lofty tone, "I'll allow my idea may be something like Bellamy's ideal society of 2000 A.D. if you'll allow *he* could have swiped his grand notion from Sir Thomas More's *Utopia*, which was copped from Plato's *Republic* and let's not worry about who *Plato* cribbed from."

Stringer laughed as loudly and about as sarcastically as London's defense plea called for. A couple of the hardcase mining men at the nearby table shot cold-eyed-curious looks his way. Stringer had long since learned how easy it was to get in trouble among hard drinkers with worried minds and perhaps a few little secrets to hide. So he glanced up at the garish Edison bulbs again to say, "Whatever they've been doing to the current here in town it seems to be all right, now, and it's way the hell past my usual supper time, Jack. What say we go scout up some beans, now that a body can navigate outside with a little light on the subject?"

London shook his head and replied, "You go ahead and grab some grub if you like. I ate earlier and, like I told you, I have a train to catch at the depot just down the way and, lights or no lights, it's still raining cats and dogs outside."

So they shook on it and Stringer rose to slip into his yellow slicker and out of that back room while the slipping was still good. He wasn't sure whether the uneasy feeling in his gut was simple hunger or some sharper instinct until, closing the door after him, he heard Big Bill Heywood rumble, "It's about time you got rid of that fink in the cowboy outfit, London. I was just about to throw the both of you out. For certain friends of the working man will be here any minute and to tell the truth I'm not too sure I even want *you* to know about 'em being here in town tonight!"

CHAPTER TWO

The storm outside had apparently blown over, so most of the crowd it had trapped out front had dissipated and it was not only possible but downright easy to belly up to the bar, now. So Stringer did, near the batwinged front entrance, to order a cigar instead of another drink on an empty stomach. He didn't smoke cigars as a rule, but he knew what the barkeep would say if he asked for a nickel bag of Bull Durham or just stood there like a big-ass bird that didn't seem to want anything at all.

What Stringer really wanted, as he went about the elaborate business of biting and lighting the two bit Havana Claro, was a clear view of that door to the back room. He knew Jack London could take care of himself in a garden variety saloon fight and it seemed as if he'd stayed back there with the boyos of his own free will. Stringer knew the erstwhile terror of the Frisco Bay oyster flats and many a hobo jungle considered himself a paid-up member of the Red Flag Fraternity. But what might the Red Flag Fraternity think of a downtrodden working stiff who'd taken of late to buying fine California estates and even fancy sailboats since he'd written all them fancy books with such big fancy words and all?

But nothing loud enough to hear out front seemed to be taking place in the back room by the time Stringer had the cigar going too good to just go on standing there without further comment. So he nodded adios at the barkeep and turned to go, just as the batwings parted to admit a lean and hungry-looking cuss with furtive eyes and a ratlike way of hugging the far wall as he darted along it to vanish through that door to the back room. Big Bill had said someone sinister seemed to be expected. Stringer just kept going with the cigar gripped between his teeth, not looking back, and heaved a sigh of relief as he got outside without anyone asking where he might be going, just as the evening was starting to get interesting. He had a pretty good notion who that rat-faced rascal had to be. He'd never seen any photographs of the one and original Albert Horsely, better known as Harry Orchard among labor organizers of the more radical stripe, but everyone from his left-wing admirers to the Pinkertons out to nail him, dead or alive, seemed to agree on that odd way he had of gliding faster on his feet without really seeming to run. If that had been Harry Orchard and not just someone trying to give the impression he was in town, then Big Bill Heywood being down here in Colorado Springs when the National Guard was hunting him in Cripple Creek made a lot more sense. Heywood's rep as a strike organizer was rugged enough. Harry Orchard didn't organize strikes. He slaughtered strike breakers. That part-time warrior over in the switchyards wasn't the only idiot in these parts talking about shooting to kill!

Out on Nevada Street the flood waters had gone down as swiftly as they'd risen and the wet paving blocks gleamed free of the usual horseshit under the electric street lamps that now shone up and down the way. Most of the downtown shops were now closed for the night, but most of the second story windows shed additional light through lace curtains or drawn blinds. Despite the earlier darkness it wasn't much later than nine and change. Stringer's empty stomach kept reminding him of that as he lingered near the next corner, undecided about his fellow member of the Fourth Estate back there. He finally decided the cigar was making him feel more butterflies under his ribs than the situation really called for. So he threw the pungent smoke in the gutter and moved on to get something more healthy to swallow. It was old Jack's own beeswax if he wanted to hang out with union toughs and mad bombers, or Knights of Labor, as some saw them. Stringer tried to keep an open mind on such matters. For in his cowhand days he'd worked for many a boss who'd deserved tar and feathers, while on the other hand they said those hardrock miners Harry Orchard had dropped down an elevator shaft along with one management man had left a heap of widows and orphans.

The streets were fairly deserted at this hour, despite the way the town was starting to dry out, but Stringer got a lady holding up a lamp post with her back to direct him to the Alta Vista Hotel and, better yet, he spied a brightly-lit chili joint ahead, even closer. So, first things coming first, he ducked inside to calm his innards with some chili con carne, coffee and mayhaps some pie with cheese, if they had either, and it was halfway fresh.

As he entered, he saw great minds seemed to run in the same sort of channels. The counter had around a dozen other late eaters seated along it. There was nowhere else to sit down in the deep but narrow interior. Stringer left his Stetson on in such informal surroundings, of course, but peeled off his crinkly and now too-warm yellow slicker to hang it up under a sign advising him to watch his hat and coat. There were six or eight other slickers already hanging there and more than one looked more expensive than his. But as he turned to grab a stool he was still pleased to note he could keep an eye on that yellow blur reflected by the silvery cookware against the back wall behind the counter. There were two Mex kids working the counter with the older and fatter short order cook. Stringer felt tempted to order in Spanish, but remembered in time that even Mexicans this far north tended to reverse the Southwestern custom of mixing Spanish in with cow talk. Growing up as he had in the cattle country of the Sierra foothills, Stringer had naturally learned to rope dally from a centerfire saddle and call what he roped with a reata. He'd been hazed unmercifully by Rough Riders from the Northern Range when he'd made that mistake while riding with them and Colonel Roosevelt in his more innocent youth. So he knew that in Colorado a reata was a damn-it rope, a sombrero was a damn-it hat, a palomino was a damn-it buckskin and anyone who pronounced Rodeo "Row-DAY-oh" like he thought he was an infernal "Matty-Door" was no-doubt a pansy who sat down to pee.

So he ordered his chili beans peppered strong enough for Texas in plain English and was served with no comment from the help or other customers. As he dug in he realized he was either hungrier than he'd thought or that the cook was really from Chihuahua. He had to keep sipping black coffee with his ferocious repast to keep from crying right out loud. Once it was down there, it sure felt swell, though. There was nothing like to to warm one's innards on a clammy night like this one. He ordered more coffee. As the nearest waiter was refilling his mug, the electric lights flicked off, went on again, and then every light within sight went off again as the Mex sighed, "Shit!" and spilled coffee all over the countertop.

Stringer had suspected he might. So he was off the stool just as a stream of scalding coffee dribbled off the counteredge all over where a slower-thinking gent's lap might have been. Stringer yelled, "Stop *pouring*, damn it!'' as he fumbled out a penny match box and struck a light. The young Mex laughed uncertainly and at least hauled the spout of his pot back far enough to wet his own toes. By this time others had thought to strike old-fashioned lights, including the fat cook, who'd turned up a gas jet above his stove to fill the interior with a flickering blue glow, growling, ''That's better. I told them they never should have taken out our old gas lamps. This electric shit never works when you really need it!''

As if to prove his point, all the Edison bulbs went back on, glowing a hesitant orange. An older man seated next to Stringer shook out his own match and announced, with a weary smile, ''I'll bet that mad scientist has come back, like they say!'' Another agreed there was no doubt about it. As Stringer got rid of his burnt out and no longer called-for match, another customer asked, in a more reasonable tone, if that thunderstorm they'd just had couldn't have done something funny to Colorado Springs' wiring. Stringer thought that made as much sense as the first old fart insisting, ''That storm blew over an hour or more ago. I tell you old Nick, the nutty professor, done something devilsome to the power plant that time he repaired it for the electric company, or said he had.''

Another disgruntled resident nodded grimly and agreed, ''Things have never worked right since they let that infernal furriner fling thunder and lightning about like he thought he was the Lord, or you know who!''

The Edison bulbs flicked off all the way, then came back on about as brightly as they were supposed to run on forty watts. Stringer reached for a napkin to do something about his sopping wet seat as he asked anyone who cared to answer, ''Did someone say the famous Doctor Tesla once worked for the electric company here in Colorado Springs?''

The old-timer who seemed to know so much shook his head and said, ''Hell, no, not even El Paso Power would have been dumb enough to pay out good money to a raving lunatic." A more reasonable old-timer had to tell the somewhat bewildered Stringer, "Professor Tesla fixed the town's main generator for 'em, free. He had to. None of us shall ever forget that wild and stormy night of the third of July in the year of our Lord, 1899!"

"He fucked up our Fourth of July entire!" chimed in yet another chili eater with an axe to grind. Stringer decided to just finish up on his feet, now that the young Mex had poured some coffee into his mug instead of aiming for his lap in the dark. The old-timer who seemed to feel their resident mad scientist hadn't been all bad was going on about the ferocious thunderstorm they'd had that wild night just before the slated festivities of the Glorious Fourth and how some said it could have just as easily been a lightning bolt as a power surge from Professor Tesla's infernal machinery when, somewhere in the night, they all heard what sounded to Stringer like a mighty fair imitation of a firing squad at work in the middle distance.

There was a thoughtful moment of silence inside the all-night beanery. Then somebody softly said, "Them was pistol shots. More than six and less'n a dozen." To which another old timer replied, as soberly, "I make it two guns, say a .44 or .45, and a smaller bore. We ought to be hearing police whistles any second, now."

He was right. As the Colorado Springs P.D. commenced to chirp back and forth up Nevada Street, Stringer spread some change on the counter and turned to grab his slicker and get back there to see if anyone he knew had just been mixed up in that shoot-out. That was when he first noticed his slicker was missing.

He stared numbly at the empty hook for a time, as it slowly sank in he'd been robbed and hadn't just done something dumb. He still looked up and down the whole wall, as if there might be a more logical explanation. When there wasn't, he announced, firmly, "Hey,

I had me an old yellow slicker hanging right under that sign advising me to keep my eye on it!''

The older gent next to him cackled, ''You should have kept your eye on it, then. I ain't got your fool slicker, cowboy!''

The others at least tried to be more helpful. When Stringer described his purloined article of rain gear and added it was worth at most two dollars and change, the old-timer who'd allowed Professor Tesla might have been innocent that time declared, ''I'm sure it had to be an honest mistake. There was a gent about your age and general size sipping coffee yonder, towards the rear of this joint. He had a *black* slicker when he come in here. That looks like it, second from the end to your left. I never saw him leave. So he must have done it during all that confusion we just had with the lights, see?''

Another customer nodded and said, ''I recall the young gent, now that I'm minded of him. He was dressed like a cowboy, too. Had on a gray hat a heap like your own, young feller. I'll bet he run out for some reason whilst them lights was out and just naturally grabbed your slicker instead of his, by mistake.''

One of the Mex kids decided, ''He'd just paid up. He was sitting there, like he was waiting for something or someone, when the lights began to flash on and off. I do not think he took your slicker for to rob you, stranger. Who but a fool would wish for to steal a slicker when the rain has stopped and he already has one of his own hanging right beside it, eh?''

Stringer moved over to finger the heavier material of the missing man's black slicker. It seemed about his size and unless the other cuss came back, pronto, Stringer figured he might be ahead of the game. Then a weary-eyed older gent wearing a derby and sporting a gilt badge on the lapel of his snuff-colored suit came in off the wet walk outside to ask, ''Might any of you gents in here be able to fill us in on a young cuss who might have passed through wearing a light gray Stetson and a bright yaller rain slicker?''

Everyone seemed to be looking at Stringer, who could only nod and say, ''We were just musing about him. You could be talking about a gent who just swapped rain slickers with me by accident. He lit out of here just a few minutes ago. Nobody here can say just where he may have headed, after that.''

The plainclothesman answered, grimly, ''I can. We just found him down by the rail depot, dead as a turd in a milk bucket with eight or ten bullet holes in the back of that yellow slicker. You say it was *your* outfit he was wearing on his way to catch a train or maybe meet someone less annoyed with him?''

Numb-lipped, Stringer reached for his billfold, as he told the lawman who he was and some grim thoughts that had just occurred to him. The plainclothesman nodded as he took Stringer's I.D. and scanned it, muttering, ''It reads either way to me, too, Mister MacKail. They might have just back-shot someone they were really after. On the other hand they were just as likely after *you* in that distinctive outfit you commenced this night in.''

The town law toted the heavy black slicker the murder victim had somehow managed to exchange for Stringer's lighter and brighter rain gear. Stringer found it enough of a chore to tote his heavy gladstone all over town for no good reason he could see. But he'd have wanted to tag along, even if he hadn't been invited to have a look-see and sign a formal deposition for the record. He'd been sent all this way to find out how serious the current labor unrest promised to be this time, and things hardly got more serious than back-shooting, no matter who the intended victim might have been.

The gent who'd died of multiple bullet wounds while wearing Stringer's yellow slicker had beaten them to the city morgue by a good twenty minutes. A three man forensic team from the El Paso County Coroner's Office had the cadaver spread out on a slanted zinc table and they were cutting him out of his damp duds as Stringer and the plainclothesman joined them in the basement autopsy theater. The first thing Stringer noticed was that he'd never seen those waxy dead features before. There was a bank of sixty watt Edison bulbs right over the strange stiff and Stringer stared down hard, from more than one angle, before he told them all, flatly, "I don't even recall him from that chili joint. Of course, if he was seated down the counter with a hat brim shading his face . . ."

The lawman who'd found the angle about yellow slickers so interesting cut in to point out, "That works two ways, MacKail. They back-shot him under a street lamp in front of the railroad depot. His face would have been shaded even better under them conditions. So the person or persons unknown threw down on that light gray Stetson and yellow slicker, not nobody's handsome profile, see?"

One of the forensic team chimed in with, "You can make that persons, *plural*, Sergeant Magnuson. We're saving the yummy parts for our boss, the deputy coroner, but the slugs that went in his back came out the front at an even wider angle. So it's safe to assume he was hit from behind and to his left by the contents of a little whore pistol, mayhaps in the delicate hands of some whore, whilst someone more manly blew rounds of .44–40 into his back from behind and to his right."

Sergeant Magnuson grimaced and growled, "Whatever. An armed and dangerous couple, strolling romantically near the railroad depot after a summer storm should have been able to get the drop on just about anyone. So the first thing we have to find out involves the I.D. of this poor dead bozo."

The helpful forensic man replied, "That's easy. He was packing a union card in his wallet." As, suiting actions to his words, he reached for a lower workbench against the wall for the wallet among the dead man's belongings they'd piled near his hat. He handed it to Magnuson, who held it up to the light and opened it to read off, "Timothy Gorman, Steam Fitter as well as paid up member of Big Bill Heywood's fucking W.F.M.!"

Another member of the team undressing the cadaver tossed in, "He was packing his own belly gun, a Harrington Richardson .32 in the side pocket of this yellow slicker. Like he might have been expecting just about what happened happening, you know?"

Magnuson turned back to Stringer, saying, "I don't think you have as much to worry about as I first feared, MacKail. We'd still better get your story down on paper for the captain to read in the cold gray dawn. Come on, we can do it sitting down in the front office."

Stringer didn't argue about that. But as he followed Magnuson up the stairwell he asked what the plainclothesman had feared so much up front.

The local lawman explained, "It still works two ways. But if Gorman was mixed up in union skullduggery the odds on him being the intended target from the beginning go way up."

He led Stringer into a side office and flicked the overhead lights on as he added, "Try her this way. Gorman knew someone was gunning for him. He was lurking in that chili joint, looking for a chance to make it out of town alive, when that power failure offered him a straw to grasp at. He swiped your yellow slicker, hoping to change his own appearance enough to make it out of town by rail."

Magnuson waved Stringer to a seat by the rolltop desk against one wall, sat himself down to haul out a pad of yellow legal sheets, and said, "It didn't work. Someone was expecting him to leave town and so they had the depot staked out. They recognized him better than he recognized them. Five'll get you ten we have a handle on it within the week. There are only two sets of suspects. Suffice it to say nobody from out-of-state with no axe to grind for either side works half as well. So let's just get your short and sweet deposition down on paper and you'll likely hear no more about it."

Stringer objected that he'd been sent to Colorado to find out as much as he could about the current unrest. But since he couldn't dig up too much dirt in a dinky office late at night, he proceeded to fill Magnuson in on the bare bones facts and figures of his past few hours in Colorado Springs. He felt no call to go into conversations he might or might not have had with gents who might or might not know any more than he did about the death of Timothy Gorman, for Jack London had assured his radical pals that he wasn't in the habit of inviting finks to even unofficial union meetings.

When the friendly and reasonable enough Magnuson asked if Stringer had noticed anyone at all sinister since his arrival, it took just a small amount of soul searching before Stringer was able to reply, honestly enough, "Save for some beligerent State Militia, I don't recall anyone who struck me as all that dangerous for a paid-up *union man* like Gorman to be around."

That seemed to satisfy Magnuson, judging by the way he went on scribbling with his pencil stub. The fact that his words were being taken down with a pencil bothered Stringer more than his conscience at the moment. For whether that had really been Harry Orchard he'd seen slithering into that back room or not, the last victim a union gun would be sent after had to be a union steam fitter on strike.

The notion of signing a deposition taken down with an easily erasable lead pencil was a lot more worrisome. He was about to voice his doubts as delicately as possible when both the overhead ceiling fixture and desk lamp blinked a few times in unison and slowly faded to yellow, then orange, to black.

"Shit, not *again*!" muttered Magnuson as Stringer got out his matches to strike a light. He was holding the tiny flame high, looking about for something more old-fashioned but reliable to light, when the juice went on again, so strong that it blew the ceiling bulb and made the desk lamp throb like a welder's arc. Magnuson mentioned shit again and added, "Let's get out of here before they damn-it electrocute the both of us. I don't know why they ever changed from gaslight to begin with. You always knew where you stood, with *gas*!"

Stringer didn't feel up to discussing the gas explosions he'd covered for his paper. He knew what Magnuson meant and had to go along with him. For he'd covered some electricated accidents since the stuff had gotten so all-fired popular and, unlike simple flood and fire, the mysterious invisible power could get downright spooky.

He just followed the plainclothesman out into the corridor, where wall lamps were blinking on and off as if they were big fireflies. Magnuson said, "I can finish your deposition from memory, once I get within range of a sensible oil lamp. Where might we be able to find you, in case the higher-ups want to pick some nits with you, MacKail?"

Stringer said he hoped to be staying at the fancy Alta Vista and that if they wouldn't let him he'd get word to Magnuson. The lawman didn't ask for further explanation. They shook on it and parted friendly as the lights winked on and off about them in a festive manner. Magnuson headed back down to watch them finish up with poor Tim Gorman. Stringer strode out the front entrance and nearly took a header down the stone steps with his gladstone when the lights inside and out went off again, and stayed off, apparently for good.

But despite all the electrical confusion, the thunderstorm that appeared to have started things on the road to ruin had long since blown over to be replaced by a starry Colorado sky, with a bright quarter moon shining down from the east to bathe everything from the slopes of Pike's Peak looming to the west to the nearest sandstone curbline in its tinfoil rays, so Stringer navigated his way to the nearest corner, got his bearings, and rolled a smoke in the moonlight as he tried to decide which way he really ought to head next.

He knew better than to seek Jack London out in that back room at this hour. But it wasn't midnight, yet, and London had said something about a midnight train to Cheyenne. He didn't think his fellow Native Son would know any more than he did about the killing of a two bit union member. But London might be able to tell him whether the one and original Harry Orchard had hung around or left that back room to perhaps hunt down other targets wearing yellow slickers in tricky light.

With the storm blown over and his original rain gear long since perforated by persons unknown, Stringer was, of course, but a long lean outline in his close-fitting denim outfit as he approached the unlit entrance of the railroad depot. So he decided, later, that it had to be his gray Stetson and the gladstone bag he was packing that inspired two barely visible boogers to step out of the inky shadows of the depot's overhang to block his way. As Stringer's gun hand swung out to hover just above his pistol grips, one of the sinister silhouettes warned him, "Don't try it, Stringer. If we meant you serious harm we'd have fired from cover. Other boys are covering us from cover, even as we speak."

Stringer nodded soberly and left his gun hand hovering right where it felt like hovering as he replied, "If all you boys are after is a conversation, what say we all go inside and enjoy a candlelight sit-down whilst we chat? To tell the truth, it makes me sort of edgy when I don't have a good view of a sinister stranger's eyes and gun hand."

His mysterious midnight conversationalist chuckled dryly and told him, "You might wind up more edgy if you knew just who you were jawing with, newspaper boy. We just have a few simple questions for you. If you answer 'em to our liking you'll be free as that other nosy pencil pusher, London, to leave this part of the world on your own living legs.''

Stringer dropped into a spread-legged stance without having to study on it as he told them both, flatly, ''Let's talk about my pal before we talk about anything else. Is he still breathing regular, inside yonder waiting room?''

The dark outline doing the talking soothed, ''Take it easy and let us not do anything tense and foolish, Stringer. London just left on the midnight flier, alive and well. It don't really pull in here from Santa Fe at midnight, but think how dumb a quarter to midnight flier would sound.''

The other looming mystery broke its silence to say in a more serious voice, ''London didn't know anything about the shooting that took place earlier just about where we're standing. When we told him about that yellow slicker he thought it was you and said dumb things about getting the son of a bitch as done a good old boy from Frisco Bay so dirty. We convinced him it would be sort of dumb to avenge the death of a trouble-maker he'd never met. He said that seeing you're still alive and, well, he's off to write about a more serious war betwixt the Japanese Mikado and the Czar Of All The Russians.''

Stringer smiled crookedly and said, ''I didn't know Russia and Japan were having trouble.'' To which his mysterious questioner replied, ''Neither did we. In any case it ain't our fight. Our fight is the coming show-down betwixt the mining men who made these mountains worth looking at and a horde of socialized Huns out to bring down the commerce of these United States in red ruin.''

Stringer nodded soberly and said, ''I take it I'm talking to the forces of law and order as the Mine Owner's Association defines the term. I heard how horrid the Western Federation of Miners was earlier this evening. The National Guard won't let me anywhere near the mines shut down by that strike, and you want me to tell you something about what might or might not be going on around here?''

The more serious of the two dark shadows said, ''We know a troublemaker named Gorman was gunned just a few yards from here as he was on his way to meet someone else, wearing your yellow rain gear in the vain hopes of throwing someone else off. After that it becomes sort of confusing. You just came from the city morgue. Who does the law have down for the likely killer, and how come?''

Stringer relaxed slightly as he detected a hint of puzzled sincerity in the mystery man's tone. Since he himself had nothing to hide, he quickly filled them in on the little he knew, and when they still seemed as puzzled he added, ''Gorman makes little sense as the victim if *neither* side did him in. You boys have no idea how comfortable that makes me feel, knowing his killers, plural, put all those rounds through the back of my very own rain slicker!''

The serious one muttered, ''All right. We know we didn't do it, and if Big Bill Heywood's started to assassinate his own followers we'll hardly need the National Guard to settle things this time. But why would anyone on either side want to blow *you* away, MacKail?''

Stringer growled, ''If I had the least notion I'd go after the bastards before they could try again! I just told you how swell it made me feel, knowing it's just as likely an innocent bystander got back-shot in my place wearing my rain gear!''

The more cheerful of the sinister pair opined, ''Tim Gorman wasn't all that innocent. As a steam fitter he had the know-how to cause real trouble, for the red flag bastards like to sabotage the machinery before they walk off the job. You might say the murder of Tim

Gorman was something like Switzerland. Wasn't it Napoleon who said that if Switzerland didn't exist someone would have had to invent it?''

Stringer replied, ''I think it was Voltaire, talking about God. But I follow your drift and I wish I could buy Gorman's killing as malice with him and no other in mind.''

The serious one said, ''We'd better break this up lest the lights go back on and make us *all* feel a mite malicious. You can go on about your business now, MacKail, as long as it's understood your business will take you out of town, if you know what's good for you.''

Stringer didn't answer. It would have been dumb to tell at least two gunslicks he didn't know on sight what he thought of their damned suggestion or, let's face it, their open threat.

CHAPTER THREE

The Alta Vista Hotel was a mite further and a heap fancier than Stringer had been led to expect. But despite his damp denim and beat-up baggage he had at least three things going for him. Jack London had telephoned the desk clerk from the depot, the lobby was dark as a crypt save for a penny candle flickering feebly here and there, and the same power failure had put their swell new Otis elevator out of service, forcing guests of any appearance to use the stairwell, so Stringer said he didn't want to wait for the bellhop, left a dime on the desk for the kid to show he was a sport, and got himself and his possibles up to Room 207 before anyone could get a good look at him.

He had to strike another match to find the room number in the dark at the head of the stairs. Then he had trouble getting Jack's key to work in the lock, until he figured out why. The door had been unlocked to begin with. He got that straightened out and ducked inside. Then he ducked even better, dropping his gladstone and drawing his .38 as he heard odd clicking and sensed movement in the blackness all about him. He froze on one knee, holding his breath, as he heard a strange voice whisper, "It's no use. They just won't work."

He sprang back up to grab blindly and, catching hold of a fistful of cloth in the dark, shoved the muzzle of his .38 against whatever he'd grabbed and snapped, "Gotcha! One false fart and you're dead!"

To which the mysterious form he was clutching replied, in a much higher tone, "Oh, Mister London, is that any way to talk to a lady?"

He laughed despite himself and started to tell her he wasn't the gent she seemed to think he was. But he figured he'd paid for his own education and didn't owe any free information to burglars of either the male or female persuasion, if that was what he'd just caught. So he growled, "Hold still and let's just pat you down for weaponry before I remove this weapon from your anatomy."

Suiting actions to his words he swung her around to shove her back against the door he'd just shut behind him, pinned her against it tight with his gun muzzle, and let go of her duds to pat her down with his free hand. She felt mighty nice. Her build was Junoesque for her height and, try as he might, he couldn't find anything on or about her soft torso that felt more dangerous than delightful. She was the one who pointed out he'd already felt for concealed weapons *there* and, come to think of it, *there* as well, so he holstered his six-gun and got out his matches to see if she could possibly look as soft and yummy as she felt.

She could. As they stared at one another rather red-faced in the matchlight, he saw she was a short busty brunette with cameo features under her upswept Gibson Girl hairdo. A middy blouse of summer weight linen would have left more of her heroic chest measurements to the imagination if their struggles in the dark hadn't popped more than one strategic button. She clutched at her gaping bodice with one hand as she became aware of a draft, or the way Stringer was staring, and protested, "Oh, look what you've done to my blouse, you brute!"

He said, "You could have wound up pistol-whipped, or worse. Didn't your momma ever warn you about sneaking into strange men's rooms after midnight, especially when they're not expecting company?"

She answered, "Pooh, I knocked on your silly door, Mister London. When there was no answer I tried the latch and when I saw you had not locked your door I felt safer inside, of course, than out there in that odious dark hallway. Didn't you get the note I left for you earlier this evening, Mister London?"

The match had burned down to where he had to shake it out and that gave him time to reconsider letting her in on a little secret. He knew he'd never seen her before. If she wasn't blind as a bat she'd seen just as much of him and yet she still had him down as a doubtless more famous newspaperman. As he struck another match and found a candle to light on the otherwise useless lamp table by the big brass bedstead, he decided to go along with the bedroom farce for now. He said, "If I'd been expecting you I wouldn't have been so surprised to find you waiting for me in the dark, Miss . . . ah?"

"Hovich, Vania Hovich, born and raised in this country but none the less at heart a Slav, like our mutual friend, Doctor Tesla!"

Stringer hung his hat on a bedpost, peeled off his damp denim jacket as well, but decided to leave his gun rig right where it was as he told her, dryly, "I didn't know I was on such close terms with old Nick Tesla, Miss Vania. Correct me if I'm wrong, but the last I read about him, in *Scientific American*, he was building this swamping tower on Long Island, back east, to compete with Professor Marconi. I'll be switched with snakes if I can figure out what either of 'em think they're up to, shooting all those sparks at the stars."

Uninvited, she sat on the bed to favor him with a puzzled smile and insist, "You have to know where he is, Mister London. Why else would you have wired him, asking for an interview regarding his more recent experiments, and why else would you have checked into the very room Doctor Tesla occupied during his earlier experiments out here near Pikes Peak?"

Stringer sat down beside her and got out the makings to give himself time to think. As he carefully rolled a smoke, going back over what little Jack London had told him about his wild goose chase, Stringer sealed the straw paper, lit the results, and thoughtfully blew some Bull Durham smoke rings before he told her, pretending reluctance, "Well, since you and your pals seem to know so much about my mysterious comings and goings, I may as well admit I hoped to catch old Nick here in Colorado Springs again, up to the same old stunts. You only have to glance at the ceiling fixture above us to see that something mighty odd has happened to the electricity in and about Colorado Springs of late. It's my understanding the power company has been trying in vain to locate the source of the trouble and, of course, we all recall how strange things got that time Professor Tesla played with artificial lightning out here, a few years back."

She said, rather severely, "It's Doctor, not Professor Tesla, Mister London. Our Croatian genius has never *taught* the subject of electricity. How could he? He's so advanced that not even Thomas Edison can follow his convoluted reasoning."

Stringer nodded and replied, "I read the mean things Edison said about Tesla and George Westinghouse during the Battle Of The Currents that was going on about the time I was enjoying the Battle of Santiago down Cuba way. Since Tesla and Westinghouse turned out to be right about Alternating Current, I'd say your point about Edison not knowing what in thunder Tesla was talking about half the time may be well taken. Let's get back to what your *Doctor* Tesla might or might not be doing to the *local* current, alternating or direct. Are you saying he did come back out here, after all?"

She sighed and replied, "We think so. Nobody knows for certain. In recent weeks certain, ah, parties have been trying to contact Doctor Tesla at his new research facilities at Wardenclyffe, Long Island. The huge tower he's built there to compete, as you put it so crudely, with that Italian upstart, Marconi, has yet to go into operation. Some of our, ah, friends who managed to pay the installation a friendly visit say that certain vital electrical gear that should be there simply isn't, as if Doctor Tesla has been, let us say, holding out on his backers?"

Stringer had no idea what sort of stuff might or might not go into a sort of Eiffel Tower designed to do Lord only knew what way the hell back east, but she seemed to think he might. So he tried, "Old Nick could be up to most anything and I doubt there's a licensed electrician born of mortal woman who could tell you what it might be. I know he made a bundle for Westinghouse the time he showed 'em how to run motors and such on alternating current, after Edison said the notion was just dumb. But haven't other backers lost a heap of money since then on some of Old Nick's more imaginative notions about talking to the folk on Mars by wireless telegraph, or running electric trains and streetcars with no wires, either?"

As if someone on Mars had been listening in, the ceiling fixture and bedlamp lit up brightly, more brightly than human eyes felt comfortable with. Stringer whistled and rose to flip off the overhead fixture. Nothing happened. He tried to switch off the bed lamp, muttering, "Here we go again. They thought they had things working right around here after they ran Doc Tesla out of town that time."

When the bedlamp refused to switch off, Stringer pulled its plug out of the wall socket. Then he scowled and meant it sincerely when he gasped, "What the hell?" For the lamp went right on burning, a lot brighter than it had been meant to burn in the first place, and Vania Hovich sounded downright triumphant as she said, "That's no short circuit the local power company has anything to say about! Only one of Doctor Tesla's wireless generators can feed power to switched off or disconnected appliances!"

The bed lamp bulb blew out with a blinding flash. The overhead bulbs faded to a dull throbbing orange. In the flickering light that made everything in the room, including them, fade in and out with a sickening strobe effect. He grabbed her to hold her still, muttering, "That can't be anyone who knows how to use Old Nick's wonderous wiring, if that's what they're doing all this with."

He noticed she wasn't really bobbing back and forth at him after all. But since she was hanging on to him as well, he didn't let go as she said, "He has to be somewhere about, as we surmised he might be. We know that when Doctor Tesla was forced to abandon his Colorado Springs experiments he left a lot of his electrical gear in storage if not simply abandoned out here. Nothing but one of his wireless generators could account for that disconnected bulb burning out like that, or the way that ceiling fixture is behaving right now!"

Stringer answered, "I've seen stage shows featuring one of those high voltage coils performing electrical wonders, but what point could a halfway sensible scientist be trying to make with all this stage magic?"

Unexpectedly, the telephone set on the other bed table rang loudly, making them both jump, albeit not too unpleasantly, since their chests bumped together. She pulled back slightly flustered, "We're only suffering the side effects. Doctor Tesla's not trying to unsettle anyone. He's just testing his wireless coils, somewhere close, one imagines."

The telephone rang some more as Stringer muttered,

"I read how he blew fuses all over town and set the main generator on fire, clear downtown, whilst he was trying to do something else entirely. But let's not worry about what Tesla or some other electified lunatic is trying to test. Let's figure out where he is, so we can ask him to cut it out before he sets the whole damned town afire this time!"

As the phone rang yet again she asked why he wasn't answering it. He growled, "I can't think of any sensible reason to. Nobody I know in town ought to know I'm here and you just saw the lamp on the other table blow out for no better reason."

But even as he groused, he reached for the infernal telephone and she didn't seem to mind when he had to lay her back across the bed and roll halfway across her to get at it. He propped the speaker as chastely as he could manage atop her well padded chest and held the hard rubber earpiece to his head, shouting, "All right, genius, you can turn your spooky spark machinery *off*, now, if you're listening at the far end of all this bodacious ringing!"

The unexpected but familiar voice of Jack London crackled back at him, "Don't shout in my damned ear, Stringer. Are you drunk or in any shape to heed your elders for a change?"

Stringer blinked in surprise and replied, "I'm not drunk. I'm just being haunted by our mutual pal, Nick Tesla. I thought that was him playing with telephone bells just now. Where are you calling from at this hour and how come?"

London told him, "Castle Rock, halfway to Denver. It's the first place I could get off to give you a holler. You've got to get *out* of there, Stringer! The balloon's about to go up and the boyos tell me they don't want any newspaper coverage of the opening rounds this time."

Stringer grimaced and said, "I think I met up with the same boyos about an hour ago. Do you know a lady calling herself Vania Hovich, blue-eyed brunette with a wasp waist but nicely padded everywhere else?''

''Stop that!'' Vania protested as he verified her dimensions below that waist cinch by rubbing his own jeans closer to her side-button skirt as, meanwhile, Jack London told him, ''The name sounds familiar, but I can't connect it up with Colorado Springs. Should I be able to?''

Stringer didn't want Vania to grab the set from him as she seemed about to. So he rolled away from her, asking London, ''Do me a favor and call me back if it comes to you, amigo. I'll likely be staying here at least until the end of the week.''

At the other end of the line Jack London swore and insisted, ''Not if you enjoy breathing half as much as I do, damn it! It's too big a boo for the space rates, cowboy! There are stories that run on the front page and there are stories that run on page three if at all. No paper as conservative as the *San Francisco Sun* is going to headline a struggle between Big Bill Heywood and the forces of Law And Order, no matter how many working stiffs get killed on either side. So why take a chance on being one of the casualties for Pete's sake?''

Stringer turned his back on the busty brunette, who seemed to be trying to tell him something, as he told London, ''Sam Barca won't let me cover the current action in the Philippines. I'm stuck with the shoot-outs he'll send me to. What's that crap you told some local gunslicks about the Russians and Japs getting set for a showdown? I heard that argument had blown over.''

London answered, ''It could be brewing up again. The Czar keeps throwing his weight around in Siberia and the Japs keep warning him he'd better pull back. Each side acts as if it thinks the other side is bluffing. So one of these days . . . Oops, there goes my train's whistle. I gotta run. Do yourself a big favor and do the same while you still can. There's no story there worth your life or, hell, even a black eye.''

Stringer tried to ask whether London had been chased out of town by the M.O.A. or his pals in the W.F.M. but he was talking into a dead line and Vania seemed to be trying to undress him, at least until she'd snatched the telephone set away from him and yelled into it in some Slavic lingo. He took it back from her, more gently, and put it aside on the bed table, saying, "It wasn't for you to begin with. Who did you think I was talking to, Doc Tesla?"

She sat up to stare down at him sort of owl-eyed, demanding, "Why were you talking about the Little Father and The Yellow Peril? Who was that, just now?"

He started to tell her the truth. Then he wondered why any news gatherer with a lick of sense would want to do a dumb thing like that.

He said, "A pal called Stringer MacKail just telephoned from up the line a piece to warn me there could be trouble brewing here in the shadows of Pikes Peak. I never would have figured that out all by myself. As for the war brewing up betwixt the Japs and Russians over Port Arthur, neither you nor Nikola Tesla look all that Japanese to me. I didn't know he was a *Russian*, though."

She almost sobbed, "The Little Father, as everyone knows, backs the Slavs of Croatia against the ambitions of the Austro-Hungarian despot, Franz Josef, and Doctor Tesla is a Croat, despite his American citizenship. So you must help me find him, Mister London! I'll do anything, anything you desire of me, if only you'll help me find Nikola Tesla in time to help my cause!"

He hauled her down beside him and bestowed a not-too-brotherly kiss upon her before he told her to just call him Jack and added, "I might be better at it if I knew more about this cause we're talking about, honey."

She started to stiffen up on him, decided to go limp in his arms instead, and confided, "The Japanese treaty with Great Britain gives their navy free access to the most modern weapons and equipment. The stupid King Edward doesn't seem to trust his own nephews, the Kaiser and the Czar, as much as he does those awful little yellow warlords!''

Stringer repressed a yawn and muttered, ''Maybe King Edward knows his own kin best. But what could trouble in the Far East have to do with trouble in the Colorado gold fields, old-fashioned *or* new?''

She snuggled closer, as if afraid of being overheard, as she explained, ''Nobody in Moscow, Tokyo or even Kansas City is apt to be helped or hurt very much by brawling mine workers. The Japanese Navy has the best wireless equipment on the international market. Thanks to the stupid British, Japanese warships can communicate in Morse code now from farther apart than they can see one another in broad daylight!''

He snuggled her closer and allowed his free hand to wander over her some, enjoying his little prank on Jack London if she wound up thinking that was the fresh cuss she was slapping, and told her he'd heard old Marconi had gotten his wireless down pretty good, these days.

She paid no attention to his roving hand as she replied, ''Pooh, Doctor Tesla has told his own backers that Marconi is a fool, barking up the wrong tree, and Doctor Tesla was right in his big feud with Edison, in case you've forgotten.''

He let his idle fingers toy with a button holding her skirt together just above what felt like a garter under the black poplin as he chuckled and answered, ''Who could forget? Edison still prefers 'Westinghouse Chair' to that electric chair they've been using instead of a gallows tree back East of late. But you have to admit Marconi's wireless sets send their dots and dashes mighty far and fast as long as there's no lightning in the vicinity.''

She said, soberly, ''Nikola Tesla has been working on a wireless system able to transmit *normal conversation* for hundreds, perhaps thousands of miles. No need to encode and decode messages as dots and dashes. It would be as if the admiral of a fleet at sea had telephone connections to all his officers as they steam into battle, see?''

He whistled softly and replied, ''An invention like that would come in so handy it sounds sort of spooky.'' But when she added that Tesla thought they'd even be able to send *pictures* back and forth by wireless some day, Stringer decided, ''Now that's just daydreaming. But whether Old Nick knows what he's up to or not, I can see a front page story in it, even if he only blows out all the fuses in town some more. So I'd be proud to help you track him down, little darling, but don't you think it's getting sort of late at night to hunt for mad or any other kind of scientists?''

She must have grasped his intent from the way he was grasping her bare thigh just inside the now open slit of her side-button skirt, for she grasped his wrist firmly to point out, ''The lights up there are still acting oddly, so Doctor Tesla must still be up and about, doing something funny, right?''

He sighed, rolled off the bed, and flipped off the wall switch. Only nothing happened. He muttered, ''When you're right you're right. Unless that coil or whatever he's fiddling with is so powerful it's downright scary, he has to be no more than a country mile from this hotel. That still leaves a heap of territory to worry about, but . . .''

The overhead bulbs flashed brighter and then went out all the way, whether the switch he'd flicked was set one way or the other. He tried the same again, with no results, as she asked, ''Didn't you say the lights had blown out all over town before, Jack?'' To which he could only answer, ''Me and my big mouth. But hold on, an overload anywhere near the generating plant could have shut off the power from here to yonder and back. Those more tricky effects you get with a high voltage coil can't have near that range or, hell, Tesla would have already made good on those offers to run electric trains all over creation without any juice hooked up to 'em directly."

He sank back down beside her, too interested in the puzzle now to worry about how much trouble he could get Jack London into with a Russian spy. He lay beside her on one elbow, musing aloud, "If only I knew where Old Nick had that tame thunder laboratory, the last time he messed up all the current in town . . ." and that seemed to inspire her to grab at him, this time, saying, "I know! I don't know if there's anything out there now, but I've seen photographs as well as a city map from the archives. The lab was, let me see, on or near the grounds of the county farm, just south of the Gold Camp Road and well up the lower slopes of Pikes Peak. I think they graze a certified herd of dairy cows there now. Cows that give milk safe for the T.B. patients at the sanitariums further up the mountain to drink, I mean."

He said, "Let's not worry about any cows that might or might not be conducting electrified experiments. If that old lab is on the Gold Camp Road, I may be able to cover two stories for the time and trouble of covering one. If anybody points a gun at me for wandering too close to what they're up to, I may just be able to convince 'em I'm nosing into something else entirely."

Then he chuckled at the picture and added, "Unless it turns out old Nick Tesla has taken sides in the miner's strike or that the boys are really striking the *power* company, that is."

She said she was going with him in the morning. He shook his head and said, "Not hardly. I can find the old Tesla lab or Cripple Creek without your help and, either way, I'd as soon have nobody else to worry about but my own fool self. So why don't we just get you on back to your own room and see if we can't both get some shut-eye, Miss Vania? It must be way past midnight by now and Cripple Creek's a good morning's ride, Lord willing and the creeks don't rise."

She said, "You have to let me come along at least as far as the old Tesla lab, then. I'm not going to let you get a wink of sleep until you promise."

He didn't want to promise any such thing. So he started fooling with her buttons some more as he growled, "Well, if you mean to spend the night here pestering me, we may as well both get some fun out of it."

She didn't argue, unless one wanted to call it a protest when she kissed him back but told him he was awfully fresh. He noticed she hadn't done anything about the buttons he'd already opened along the side of her skirt. So he took advantage of that advantage and when it developed she wasn't wearing anything under her outer duds, betwixt her gartered silk stockings and black waist-cinch, Stringer just did what seemed most natural at such times and though she seemed to be welcoming him with yawning thighs, she suddenly gasped, "Oh, Jack, what's *happening*?" as he began to enter her and did some gasping as well. Aside from the way her moist innards seemed to tingle, he couldn't help noticing that every hair on her head had come unpinned to stand up straight and, worse yet, snap and crackle in a big halo all around her head. She yelped that he'd shocked her just awful when she tried to move his jeans down further off his bare buttocks and when he reached down to do it right he swore like a trooper and told her, "Jesus H. Christ! You're right! One or more of us seems to be wired a.c., d.c., or both!"

There were times for sex and there were times for electrical experiments. He rolled off her and shucked every stitch he had on, telling her to do the same. He could see she was doing as he'd asked her to. He could *hear* it, too, for as she rolled her silk stockings down they gave off harmless but still astoundingly bright sparks!

She whimpered, "What on earth is happening to us, Jack?" as he lay her back across the linen sheets after shucking the silk-covered counterpane and braced his bare feet against the brass rails at the foot of the bed. He reentered her, this time without shocking her exactly the same way, and told her, with a chuckle, "That was high voltage indeed, mayhaps from a static generator you can buy in kit form to impress the neighbors. Some silly rascal on or about the premises has a hell of a static field going, but since I'm grounded to a hundred pounds or more of brass and neither one of us is in contact with silk, or amber, or such . . ."

"My hair still feels tingly." She cut in. So he told her, "Hair's close to silk and we're way above sea level in thin air that's inclined to make your hair sparkle in any case. Don't worry about it. Nobody's trying to electrocute anyone. But if he doesn't cut it out he's sure to get *caught* any minute."

"You know where he's running that mysterious spark coil, Jack?" she asked, adding, "Let me get on top if you'd rather chat than move the way I like it, darling."

He started to move in her the way he assumed they both liked it. Then he wondered why he'd want to be so beastly to a lady who'd asked so politely and, as they changed positions on the bed, he assured her, soothingly, "I don't have to figure out where the idiot and his demonstration gear might or might not be. He's messed up all the juice in town for hours, now, and there has to be more than one crew of troubleshooters out there trying to trace the short circuits. I'm sure they know a heap more than you or me about the care and feeding of their county-wide power circuits. So let's just enjoy the tingle our own way, while we can." To which she coyly replied, "I don't feel any electrical field now, darling. I'm doing that down there myself." And all he could say was, "I know. Don't stop. This is one pleasure modern science will never be able to improve!"

CHAPTER FOUR

Vania was a sport about it, once she recovered from the shock of having gone to bed with Jack London only to wake up in the morning feeling used if not abused by some other newspaperman entirely.

Knowing she'd have to be told sooner or later, if only as a common courtesy to the real Jack London, Stringer had waited until about as late as he dared and, knowing something about cold gray dawns, waited until he had her almost ready to come some more before he'd let her in on it, so after cussing him and begging him for more at the same time Vania had apparently decided no man who could make a lady come that hard could be all bad and, what the hell, she confided coyly, a newspaperman in her bush was worth two that couldn't find Doctor Tesla for her any better.

Since she told him this fondly as they were sharing a warm shower and hot sex in the adjoining bath, Stringer suspected Vania knew as much as he did about timing one's words with one's actions. So, not wanting an argument at a time like *this,* for God's sake, he just kissed her a lot and allowed he'd sure keep an eye out for old Nick as he went about his other morning chores, provided she let him get dressed this side of noon.

She must have wanted him to scout Tesla up for her and her Czar, for it wasn't quite nine thirty by the time Stringer made it over to Nevada and Platte with a fair breakfast filling his innards above the belt and everything below the belt feeling just a mite drained.

Once more in control of his own movements, near the center of town, Stringer picked up some Bull Durham and directions at a corner tobacco shop, bought himself a new slicker, and hired himself a livery mount and stock saddle at the rather dear price of six bits a day plus deposit.

The new slicker was charcoal black and neither as light nor as bright as the one he'd lost. His reasons for switching to rain gear nobody'd ever noticed him wearing before were as obvious as they might have been uncomfortable and, what the hell, outside it didn't look as if it was fixing to rain right now.

The livery pony, chosen with the same considerations in mind, was a nondescript bay gelding that could have passed for being part mule if such bloodlines had been possible. The saddle was a double-rigged roper, complete with a sixty or seventy-foot coil of grass rope.

Stringer felt no call to comment on a livery saddle gussied up so functional. He assumed they'd bought the saddle cheap as well as used off some hard-up working hand and while Stringer had been raised in Centerfire Saddle country, to rope dally style with a braided reata in chaparral that precluded such long tie down ropes, whether grass or rawhide, he could rope High Plains style if he had to, knew he wasn't likely to have to, and felt he'd blend in better on the trail if he was traveling with a serious-looking stock saddle as well as Stetson, spurs and such. For since even before the turn of the century a heap of nesters, townsmen and even easterners had taken to dressing up cowboy-style whilst riding anywhere out West. Word had no doubt spread that certain hands with nothing better to do enjoyed rawhiding dudes. Meanwhile anyone with a lick of common sense could see the work duds of Cattle Country were most practical under the conditions one was most apt to encounter in the more primitive parts of the West. Save for a few trimmings, nothing much a real cow hand wore had ever been designed just to slow a man of action down.

With his new slicker tied across the saddle bags behind him, and said saddle bags packing provisions for a longer trip than he really intended, Stringer rode for Cripple Creek, trying to look more like a local cow hand hunting strays than an out-of-state newspaperman hunting a story some might not want to see printed.

The Gold Camp Road had to do some climbing, almost from the start. While the highest crest of Pikes Peak terminates a good ten miles west of Downtown Colorado Springs, it does so fourteen thousand feet and change above sea level. So to get there the ground has to start sloping just west of Fountain Creek and well inside the city limits.

Thus it came to pass that Stringer and his livery mount were well above the roof tops to their east when they came upon the oncemore quiet cow pasture Nikola Tesla had raised so much Ned in just a few short years before. The dairy herd was grazing, apparently untended, on the grassy slopes inside the three-strand barbed wire fence that ran alongside the Road. Near a gate on the upslope edge of the vast clearing Stringer spied a handful of frame buildings clustered around the base of a truncated timber tower. It reminded him of the oil derricks sprouting west of the Mississippi since the Spindletop Dome in Texas had proven there was rock oil out this way after all. The timber tower sprouting from this cow pasture had obviously been bigger, in its time. It was just as obvious a lot of the timber had been salvaged. So while the structure could have risen as high as three hundred feet in its day, they'd cut it down to no more than a three or four story stump since then. The buildings Tesla and his crew had used not all that long ago, had been worked over by the bone pickers as well. He saw a buckboard parked in front of the biggest barn-like structure, a swaybacked but still living draft critter. So Stringer reined in, tethered his own pony to a gate post, and rolled through the wire to mosey over and have a friendly word or more, he hoped, with whoever might have beat him out here this early in the morning.

As he approached the stripped-down lab, an older man wearing whipcord pants and lace-up boots under a sort of baseball cap and rough blue workshirt came out, looking disgusted until he spotted Stringer and decided to look more like a wooden Indian.

Stringer kept walking without breaking stride or swinging his gun hand anywhere near his right hip until, at conversational range, he called out, "Morning. Might you be in charge of those fine dairy cows?"

The stranger shot a morose glance at a contented looking deer-colored Jersey grazing just down the slope as he told Stringer, "I was fixing to ask you the same, cowboy. I answers to Fletcher, Sparks Fletcher, and my chosen occupation would be troubleshooting for the Electric Company."

Stringer allowed he'd noticed they had some trouble worth shooting and, after introducing himself and stating his own business, told the electrician, "Great minds seem to run in the same channels. Is this where Doctor Nikola Tesla played with lightning bolts that time?"

Fletcher nodded grimly and replied, "It was. Don't ask me what he and them other infernal furriners figured they was *doing* up here. I only worked with the crew as run a plain old hundred and ten volt utility line this far to 'em. Hotwire Hamilton, the only licensed electrician from town that Tesla had working for him, swears that Tesla could crank the juice up past a million volts, and Lord knows how high they got her the night that Croation asshole blew every damn fuse in the county by running our main generator *backwards*, on *lightning* power, 'til it just naturally melted and set the whole damn plant on fire!''

Stringer nodded soberly and got out his note book as he said, ''I heard a lot of folk out here were sort of vexed with Old Nick and his experiments. Seeing you're the first paid-up electrician I've been able to ask, have you any notion just *why* Tesla felt the need to haul down lightning from the sky?''

The older man grimaced and replied, ''*Loco en la cabeza,* most likely. Both Marconi and Edison are on record, now, as having allowed in as gentle a manner as possible that Tesla's notions of invisible electrical rays don't jibe with any *they* can get to work.''

Stringer sighed and said, ''You're already over my head, Sparks. I know the heavy thinkers have been playing with invisible rays since at least the late 1880s, but I'll be scalded with sheep dip if I know what they're talking about. I took General Science in High School. So I think I know how a wet cell makes an Edison bulb glow. But please don't ask me why dipping two kinds of metal in acid creates an infernal electric current to begin with.''

Sparks chuckled and assured him, ''Don't worry. I don't have the time, even if you had the interest, and there are too damn many licensed electricians in the city directory as it is.''

Stringer cocked an eyebrow and asked, ''Did you just say one such gent named Hamilton worked for Doc Tesla in the flesh out here?''

Fletcher nodded and said, ''I'd hardly call old Hot-wire a gent, but she's in the directory. I already asked her if she's seen hide or hair of any of the old bunch this summer. But she tells me she's sure her old boss is playing with lightning back east on Long Island and . . .''

"Hold it." Stringer cut in, even as he wrote the name down, but demanded, "Are you saying one of the electricians Tesla hired to help him out here was a *woman*?"

Fletcher nodded and explained, "Widow woman. Kept the business going when her man Westinghoused his fool self with 800 Volts, a.c. She's in the book and it's a free country, but I doubt old Hotwire can tell you who or what's been screwing up our system for weeks. Like I said, I asked her if she knew and she told me all she knew was that she's been busy as hell fixing burnt-out appliances. We keep telling folk not to replace burnt-out fuses with copper pennies but they just won't listen and you ought to see what a power surge can do to a lady's hair curling iron or, for that matter, a lady curling her hair, at such wonderous times!"

Stringer grimaced and replied, "Jesus, has anyone been electrocuted by these mysterious modern wonders, Sparks?"

Fletcher shook his head, albeit dubiously, and said, "It's only a question of time, if we don't get a handle on the matter, pronto. If it was up to me alone we'd just pull the plug and let folk do with coal oil and candles 'til we could trace the whole damn county grid from steam boilers to last outlying street lamps. But, considering how short a time we've had enough electric juice to matter, a heap of folk have grown dependent as hell on it. It ain't just fear of the dark that causes panic every time the power fails us. Now that we got things from street cars to hotel elevators running with electric motors . . ."

"It's a pain in the ass and even front page news." Stringer cut in, adding, "Or it would be, if I could file more in the way of cause and effect. You say you're sure the trouble's not originating at the generating plant, itself?"

Fletcher looked injured and replied, "Bite your tongue. Where in tarnation did you expect us to start tracing the circuits from, the top of yon Pikes Peak? You're as bad as that infernal Hotwire Hamilton, herself. She as much as accused the company of plotting to burn out all the fuses in town just so we could sell fresh ones to all our customers."

"Does the local power trust sell gas and electric appliances as well?" asked Stringer, making a shorthand note as he waited for an answer. Sparks shrugged and answered the question with a question, asking, "Don't tobacco shops sell matches?" Then he spoiled it all by adding, "You can buy fresh fuses, light bulbs and such at the same office where you pay your electric bill. The company offers its customers a real bargain, selling at cost just to keep everyone using plenty of juice. Every other outlet in the county has to charge twenty to forty percent more. That's how come Hotwire spoke so spitefully. She knows we don't make any real profit underselling her on damned light bulbs. Even if we did, we lose a bundle every damn time all the lights go out. For we bill customers by their meters and the damn meters don't *run* when the power is off!"

Stringer stared thoughtfully at the ramshackle shed the trouble shooter had come out of, saying, "There has to be a less complicated way to peddle nickel fuses and two bit light bulbs. What were you expecting to find out here in the way of electrified skullduggery, Sparks?"

The older man sighed and said, "I hope I'll know it when I see it. I don't see how you can switch current off and on without no switch. I recalled a swamping switchboard they had in yonder shed when Doc Tesla was playing The Great Jehova out here that time. But they've about stripped out everything but a bolt here and a brass tack there."

Stringer glanced up at the sky, noting the way the morning sun had risen whilst he could still see the rooftops of the city sprawling off to their east, and allowed it was a pure puzzle, but that he still had to get on over to Cripple Creek some time that day. So they shook on it and parted friendly.

Stringer hadn't ridden much farther west when the road cut sharply south to follow a contour line around the southeast apron of Pikes Peak. Stringer didn't argue. The road was still taking him skyward at a fairly wearisome grade. It was a funny thing, or would have been a funny thing to anyone less used to riding through high country, that this close to a mountain it got tougher to see the mountain. Gazing upslope once you were up the slope a ways, you had so many lesser bulges between you and the peak that the higher you went up a mountain the lower and less impressive it seemed. It was only when he gazed the other way, out across the rolling prairies to the southeast, that he could see how high he was now, even though the grass and gravel to either side of the road didn't appear to slope this far down from the serious heights.

He was just getting used to the way the road seemed to gently wrap around the mountain, when he rode around a house-high outcropping and felt his heart skip a beat as his pony seemed to take wing and fly like Pegasus across the Colorado sky for a spell. Then Stringer saw they were still trotting along on solid ground,. where the mountain road had been cut into an almost sheer cliff by some infernal engineer with a heap of dynamite and a lot more optimism than Stringer might have had faced with a damned wide canyon to cross.

There wasn't any way to cross such a wide gulf, so after scaring Stringer good, the road hairpinned away from the drop-off to enter a deep dark tunnel blasted through solid granite. This naturally spooked the flying horse more than it did its human rider. So Stringer had to dismount and lead or, more to the point, *drag* the reluctant steed into what it likely took for a dragon's lair.

It was just as well he'd done so, he felt sure, when halfway through the tunnel, just as Stringer had assured his fool mount on the scarcity of horse-eating dragons on the slopes of Pikes Peak, they were beset by a roaring, honking, glary-eyed monster or mayhaps a horseless carriage, tearing up the road and into the tunnel after them at the scorching speed of twenty damned miles an hour!

The livery bay tried to buck off its rider and bolt, which may have been rougher on Stringer if he hadn't already been afoot with a good grip on the reins. He clapped his free palm to the bay's muzzle to calm it, or strangle it into submission, by covering its flared nostrils with a firm palm. For, unlike humans and most other critters, horses can't inhale through their mouths and, since they *know* this, they know better than to argue with the smaller species than long ago outsmarted them, unless, of course, a human is dumb enough to give them an even break.

"Asshole!" Stringer hollered at the driver, if any, of the fancy black and tan Panard as it whipped through the scant space between him, his pony, and the far wall.

"Fuck you!" a cheery voice echoed through the tunnel amid the popcorn rattle of its tinny engine and the rumble of its red rubber tires over loose gravel. Stringer coughed dust, swore some, and led his now really spooked pony on until they were out in the sunlight again, with the road once more to themselves, albeit dust was still settling up ahead.

Stringer remounted and rode on, putting the rude road hog out of his mind as, for the first time since leaving town, the scenery began to get downright pretty.

This far from town the slopes had been left to their original appearance, with second or even first-growth timber shading the road and cutting the thin dry winds that could goosebump you by surprise at any time up here, if they caught you in the open. Some of the trees were aspen, lodgepole and other scrub species that you found after mankind or wildfire had passed through.

But further from the roadway he spied downright impressive fir and spruce. Orchard grass grew emerald green between the tree trunks with wild flowers, mostly yellow and lavender, indicating nobody much could be living hereabouts. For while menfolk could live and let live around wild flowers, there was some mysterious inner urge that possessed women as well as children and pack rats to reach for anything shiny or brightly colored.

Stringer, having long since decided pretty things looked as pretty where they grew naturally, was content to just enjoy the ride as it turned out nicer than he'd expected. He rolled a smoke, made dead certain his match was out before he tossed it away amid such pretty scenery, and hadn't been smoking long before they rounded a bend to see yet another tunnel ahead. The little strip of Rocky Mountain greenery, like so many of life's other pleasures, had been just a brief surprise. He had to get back down and drag his damned mount through again. Things went on that way for the next few hours. Then he noticed the grade was taking them ever lower instead of higher and, again, the slopes all about got bleak and bare, with an old tree stump rotting here and there to explain why. Mining took a heap of timber for pit props and there were a heap of mines in the gold fields up, or actually down, ahead.

There wouldn't have been enough timber on all of Pikes Peak to supply the many mines of Teller County this late in the game. That was why the surrounding stumps were so old. Everything from pit props to potatoes for some time had had to be shipped in bulk to the barren and bleak but still mighty prosperous gold fields.

Stringer had done some background reading on the train from San Francisco. So he knew an elder race of American explorers had discovered Pikes Peak long before Zebulon Montgomery Pike had put the mighty monadnock or isolated massif on the white man's map.

The Mountain Utes insisted the creation of their known

world had begun there, for anyone with a lick of sense could see how all the rocks and mud that rose above the original Great Bitter Water must have cascaded down through one hole in the sky, above such an obvious center of the world, to spread out in every direction, like a big buffalo turd.

The Arapaho, who'd guarded its eastern slopes more ferociously, insisted the Utes were full of it and that Ma'tou, The Great Medicine, had given them the vast triangle bounded by the Shining Mountains, the Platte to the north and Arkansas to the south as their Happy Hunting Grounds on Earth. Only, the First Ones, weary of even easy hunting and food gathering, had decided they'd rather go on to the Ghost World, where things were even better.

So they'd gathered all their medicine things together, including good earth, rock, seeds and such, and gathered on a high place to demand entry through the Sun Door, no doubt raising an awful din with all their chantings and thumpings until Ma'tou, pissed off at their noise and ingratitude, had let out such a roar that all the First Ones had dropped everything they owned in one big pile, which was, you guessed it, the impressive bump the pale faces called Pikes Peak.

Left to local Indian legends and Zeb Pike's laconic notations nothing more significant might have occurred in the Pikes Peak Country if a Cherokee guide called Falling Leaf hadn't wandered into Leavenworth, Kansas, with an eagle quill of gold dust, panned, he said, in the Front Range of the Shining Mountain.

Falling Leaf falls through a crack in history after getting into a nasty, if not fatal, saloon brawl he had to be carried away from. But word was out. There was gold in the Front Range, *some* damned where, and any fool could see Pikes Peak was as impressive as the Front Range got. So it was "Pikes Peak Or Bust!" and a lot of folk got busted. The Shining or Rocky Mountains extend one hell of a ways north and south, a heap of them rise higher than Pikes Peak, and there's no reason gold, heavier than lead, should flow uphill to begin with. As a matter of fact, gold was found lots of other places before it came to pass that in the Year Of Our Lord, 1878 a rancher with a drinking problem and the handle of Bob Womack was riding along the rocky banks of Cripple Creek, just southwest of Pikes Peak and so-called because an earlier explorer's pony had busted a leg trying to ford the boulder-haunted white water.

Stringer suspected the tale was too pat to be true, but legend had it that good old Bob wasn't searching for color aboard his pony, Old Whistler, that brisk May morn. He'd taken to hiding a little brown jug in the creek, out of sight of his modest homespread, to keep his medicinal red-eye cool and safe from confiscation by Eliza, A.K.A. Miss Liza, who was Womak's spinster sister, common law wife or, as the least charitable version would have it, both. All versions agreed Miss Liza just couldn't abide Bob's drinking. Hence the need for the little brown jug in Cripple Creek, leading, of course, to his inevitable discovery of a big slab of float, or gold ore from somewhere higher up.

That was where the story should have had its happy ending, had it been cut from whole cloth. But while the float he'd found assayed at $200 a ton, good old Bob never *found* a ton, and soon became known as "Crazy Bob", driven now by dreams as well as hard liquor to neglect everything in search of the Mother Lode or source of that teasing chunk of High Grade. Soon literally busted by Pikes Peak, Womack was forced to sell off the land he'd inherited from his more ambitious father. Unable to hold a job because of his drinking and monomania about that one bit of color he'd found, Crazy Bob somehow survived until the fall of 1890, a dozen years later, when, to everyone's astonishment but his own, he struck the El Paso Lode, a two-foot thick vein of gray volcanic rock all the experts had already dismissed as the wrong kind. It assayed at $250 a ton and there were obviously a heap of tons under a fifteen-hundred foot long claim he'd staked out near the confluence of Cripple Creek and Poverty Gulch. But, strange as it must have seemed to poor old Crazy Bob, nobody seemed to *give* a fig. The smart money boys had been warned by the experts that even if there should be gold in such unfamiliar rock, there was no assurance the infernal stuff could be refined by existing methods and, in any case, hadn't the stuff been found to begin with by that Crazy Bob Womack?

In the end, the weak and unfortunate Womack had been forced, or felt he'd been forced, to sell his claim to a Colorado Springs druggist named Grannis for $300 and, legend had it, a bottle of Jack Daniels.

John Grannis had likely felt he was being charitable. He'd backed Crazy Bob before to the tune of a hundred or so and may have felt he was throwing good money after bad when nobody seemed to want to buy his hard gray rock, and other prospectors, with better reps than Crazy Bob's, proceeded to go broke digging gold ore, good gold ore, from the southeast slopes of Pikes Peak.

As a Californio, Stringer understood there was so much more to producing gold than simply finding it. As many a buyer of gold mining stock had learned the hard way, it was easy to lose money really digging gold. It wasn't worth much mixed with rock. Refined to 24 karat bullion, the U.S. Mint would take it off your hands at circa $20 an ounce. The problem was producing an ounce of pure gold at less cost to you and your stockholders than circa $20. It wasn't as easy as it sounded, once you started paying all the bills a going gold mine racked up, whether it was producing or not.

Stringer wouldn't have been riding for the Cripple Creek gold fields, of course, if things had stayed as grim as they'd turned out for Crazy Bob Womack, Charly Cocking and dozens of other hollow-eyed prospectors who, all told, never ripped $300,000 from the hard gray ore of Cripple Creek with the ball-busting methods of the old fashioned gut-and-gitters. The rich but stubborn high temperature ore only yielded its treasures to the most modern and hence expensive refining methods, which led in turn to the takeover of the Cripple Creek area by the Robber Barons, or "Financiers" as they preferred to be called.

Stringer knew that, to be fair, many of the bigwigs President Teddy Roosevelt now cussed as "Millionaire Malefactors" had started with less jingle in their jeans than old Silver Spoon Teddy to begin with. So he was less ready to cuss a man who'd made more than he had before he knew just how the rich cuss had wound up so rich. But as he rode around a bend to spy what blocked the road just ahead, he was ready and able to cuss considerable. Then he had to grin. For that black and tan horseless carriage that had almost run him down and told him to fuck himself was stalled on a stretch of level grade and, better yet, the sissy-dressed dude who'd been burning up the road so high and mighty was standing there like a big-ass bird in his high-button shoes, canvas duster and peaked tweed cap with goggles strapped to it. As Stringer rode closer, he saw the cuss was older and more red-faced than himself. The stranded motorist glared up at Stringer to announce, "So help me, God, if you tell me to get a horse I mean to kick the shit out of you!"

Stringer doubted the older and softer-looking gent was up to such a chore, but he'd been raised to speak respectful to his elders, if they'd let him. So he just said, "You more likely need to set your carburetor richer, amigo," to which the obviously richer man replied, "What are you talking about, cowboy? What in the hell is a carboneater and do you know what could be wrong with the son of a bitch in any case?"

Stringer reined in to reply, "Despite the cowboy duds, I know a little about gasoline engines, amigo.

They drive 'em, some, where I bed down betwixt more rustic chores. I don't know why I ought to help such a rude old rascal clear this public thoroughfare of fancy French scrap metal, but if you promise not to beat me up, I may be able to fix your fool machine for you."

The rich dude looked a heap friendlier than he had up to now, as he assured Stringer it was worth fifty dollars to him if he could make it on down to Cripple Creek before suppertime.

Stringer glanced at the sky, muttered, "Hell, Cripple Creek can't be that far," and dismounted, adding, "I need a screwdriver." When the fool mountain-motorist naturally moaned he didn't seem to have any tools aboard his Panard, added, "Never mind. If my jack knife won't do it I likely don't know what I'm doing to begin with."

The rich dude watched with a certain interest tempered with suspicion while Stringer opened the hatch exposing the compact air-cooled engine, explaining, "They make these machines in France, which can't get half as high as Colorado, and, we're way higher than even Denver right now. So your engine has to have either more air, which it can't get at this altitude, or more fuel, which we ought to be able to manage, once I figure out just how this French carburetor works."

The owner of the suffocated horseless carriage kept asking dumb questions as Stringer tinkered with its innards. Stringer wouldn't have minded answering, had the old fart known one infernal thing about the way his expensive toy worked. But like a spoiled kid playing with a wind-up tin merry-go-round, up to now he'd apparently never cared, as long as it *worked*.

Stringer figured he had the carburetor set richer and told the dude to get in and man the throttle and spark whilst he gave the old engine a crank. Stringer wasn't expecting the Panard to start on the first try, but it seemed a good old machine, once you gave it something to run on. It started on the first crank and hummed like a sewing machine as the driver spun its rear wheels in the gravel to take off down the road, calling back, "So long, Sucker!"

Stringer shrugged and plucked the reins of his mount from the dust to remount, muttering, "Poor bastard. Having enough money to know he won't starve after all seems to have gone to his one brain cell."

Then he rode on, rolling another smoke as he walked his pony down the gentle slope. He told it, "I've been rich and I've been poor, and rich is better, Brownie. But let's hope we never get rich enough, or poor enough, to turn mean. That poor bastard's no doubt so used to paying for everything, including a kiss from his own wife, that he figures everyone he meets is out to skin him and, being he's such a miserable old fart, they likely *are*."

He was more interested in finding Cripple Creek than he was in old farts in motor cars, so he'd about forgotten the incident when he rode around yet another bend to find his tormentor parked ahead, with his motor mysteriously running this time. As Stringer rode closer, wearing a bemused smile, the rich old dude smiled back, in a surprisingly boyish manner, to ask, "What's the matter with you, cowboy? Don't you have no temper at all? Most men would have gotten sore and pegged a shot, or at least shaken a fist, back yonder."

Stringer chuckled fondly and replied, "Well, hell, if you really want me to turn you over my knee and give you a good spanking, you know I'm as ready as most to do another wayfaring stranger a favor."

The older man stared up thoughtfully to say, "That's my point. You don't know who I am, do you?" To which Stringer could only honestly reply, "Nope, and to tell the truth I don't much give a shit. The longer I know you the less I want to, you poor miserable cuss."

The motorist drew himself up imperiously to announce, "I don't feel all that miserable, cowboy. It so happens you have the honor of addressing T.S. Murdstone of Murdstone Minerals Incorporated!"

Stringer shrugged and replied, "Then I'd be S.K. MacKail of the *San Francisco Sun*. What does T.S. stand for, Tough Shit?"

"Thomas Stanhope," snapped the rich dude, adding, "You must not know who I am, after all."

Stringer shook his head and answered, "I know who you are. I still don't give a shit. I'm not looking for a position as a hired gun or, God forbid, a strikebreaker, so you being a big shot in the Mine Owners Association don't cut no ice with me. As for the fifty bucks you welshed on, I never asked shit for a simple enough favor and if it makes you happy, thinking you outsmarted me, feel free to jerk off with all fifty dollars wrapped around your dong. Just don't mess with me no more. I mean that. You're commencing to piss me as much as a fly buzzing around under my hatbrim might."

He would have ridden on. But Murdstone almost pleaded, "I want to ante up, damn it. I only spun out like that back yonder to see how you'd take it."

Stringer said, "I told you how I'm starting to take you and your rich-kid notions, Tough Shit. I don't want your money. I doubt I'd even want your sister if she was half as stuck-up-piggy-looking as you."

He rode on. Murdstone threw his Panard in low gear to tag along beside him, calling up, "Hey, look, I was out of line and I'm sorry, all right?"

Stringer smiled down, more pleasantly, and decided, "Sure. Forget it. We all have our bad days and I'm willing to call it a draw if you are."

He meant it. Murdstone said so and seemed surprised, even as he said so. He hesitated, then said, "Look, I owe you and there's something you might not know about the road further down the damn mountain."

Stringer allowed he was listening. Murdstone said, "You can't get through to Cripple Creek, the way you seem to be trying. The Colorado Guard has set up a brace of Browning machine guns as well as a lot of bob wire. You weren't the first one to mention hired guns or strikebreakers in connection with Cripple Creek, see?"

Stringer said, "I do now. I was sent here by my paper to cover such festivities. I thank you for the tip and I reckon I'll just have to ride around the chocolate soldiers after sundown."

Murdstone shook his head and said, "Less, ah, regular gunhands posted on the slopes to prevent just that will pick you off for sure if you act half that sinister."

Stringer swore and muttered, "Damn it, there has to be *some* way I can cover Cripple Creek for my paper. It says so in the Constitution." To which T.S. Murdstone answered, with just a hint of oil in his tone, "I can get you through the military roadblock, easy. Provided you're willing to, ah, grant me one more little favor."

Stringer said, "Let's hear it. I ain't about to bend over for the soap, but, otherwise, we can likely work something out."

Murdstone nodded and said, "You may have noticed I don't know too much about these here internal combusted engines." To which Stringer felt it best to reply with no more than a sardonic nod. So T.S. continued, "A certain business rival of mine just bought a robin's egg blue Buick runabout and, worse yet, knows more than me about motor cars and tends to brag about it beyond human endurance."

"You want me to let the air out of his tires?" Stringer asked with a dubious frown, which made Murdstone laugh like a mean little kid and say, "Not hardly. I want you to fix this Panard so's it can climb Pikes Peak, all the damn way to the top!"

Stringer swung in his saddle to stare soberly north, although he couldn't see halfway to the summit because of the lesser but closer bulges between. He said, "I dunno, T.S. one can see from down in Colorado Springs that the mountain's sloped steep and sort of Alpine-like to the north but takes a more gentle slope to the south. I doubt you'd need a rope and such just *walking* up the south slope but a horseless carriage, up a damn mountain . . . ?"

"There's both a wagon trace and a cog railroad to the summit," Murdstone cut in, explaining, "The Pikes Peak Railway has been traipsing tourists to the top in tilt-built cars since the summer of '91. The wagon trace had to be laid out first, for any railroad work to get done. Lots of folk have made it to the top every whichway, save by horseless carriage, if you follow my drift."

Stringer did. But he asked, "Don't you and the other mining moguls have more to worry about than bragging on mountain climbing motor cars, what with your big miner's strike and all?"

T.S. looked sincerely puzzled as he replied, "Why should we be worried? We *own* the mines and, if the truth be known, most of the miners, along with their wives and daughters if we wasn't so particular. That loco anarchist Big Bill Heywood is just beating his head against a brick wall with his talk of the owners having to pay the medical bills of careless mine workers. We have three-quarters of the union rank and file down in the shafts where they belong and there are plenty of ambitious lads willing to take their places as Heywood can talk 'em into walking off their job and out of their company housing while they're at it. Meanwhile, all the mines in and about Cripple Creek are producing as much ore as they did before Heywood *called* his fool strike, and life must go on. If you was to rig that carburetor thing on my engine right, do you reckon I could drive this critter to the tippy-top of this here mountain?"

Stringer shrugged and said, "I could try. I'm no automotive engineer, but it does seem to me a machine this light and frisky ought to be able to go most anywhere a steam locomotive can get to, with or without a cogged track. It's just a matter of keeping the engine turning over as the air thins out up yonder, see?"

T.S. didn't, really, but he chuckled and said, "I want you down in Cripple Creek, then. I'll get you through the guard and them fool machine guns. You'll even be free to write about the labor situation for your yellow journal, for *my* side has nothing to hide. The only string I insist on is that you'll be at my beck and call when, not if, I can get a little wager down on this Panard's ability to climb Pikes Peak. Agreed?''

Stringer nodded and said, ''Sure. Why not? But how are we to work it, you being on those red rubber wheels and me being on this pony and all? Do you reckon we could tether the critter to your trunk rack and lead him down the slope in mighty low gear?''

T.S. Murdstone grimaced disdainfully and said, ''I have neither the time nor the patience to spare. I'll just write you out a military pass and you can follow me down to Cripple Creek at your own equestrian pace, MacKail.''

As he reached under his duster for an officious-looking pad and a gold plated fountain pen, Stringer felt obliged to ask, ''How come you get to issue military passes, you being a civilian and all, as far as I can see. Might you be some sort of reserve officer, T.S.?''

Murdstone looked disgusted and began to write direct orders to the National Guard as he replied, downright smugly, ''I'm more important than any fool officer or, hell, Governor Peabody, for that matter. He takes his orders from me and, naturally, his soldiers take their orders from him. Don't strain your brain over it, Stringer. Nobody will mess with you as long as you got *me* backing you. I hope you savvy that applies vice versa, newspaper boy.''

CHAPTER FIVE

Cripple Creek, more or less centered on the original Poverty Gulch Lode, was the most substantial but hardly the only settlement in the gold fields spattered over the southwest shirttails of Pikes Peak. For gold was where one found it and gold, along with silver, had spawned the satellite settlements of Altman, Independence, Victor and, of course, Goldfield.

Long before you got near any of 'em, the heavy hand of humankind and the hooves of overgrazing livestock had turned the normally timbered slopes to stony desert, and muddy gullies ran along the rocky beds of long-dead trout streams. But while the original trees were long gone, a line of creosoted utility poles ran between the wagon trace and the railroad that joined it north of Cripple Creek, where outcrops of bedrock formed a natural bottleneck. So they'd posted proclamations of martial law, printed on heavy stock, every third or fourth pole, all bearing the same message. Neither Governor Peabody, nor General Bell, wanted anybody visiting the goldfield without a mighty good reason they approved of personally. Such sissy notions as Trial By Jury and Habeas Corpus were suspended during the current state of "Anarchist Agitation", as the State of Colorado saw anything that slowed down production in a part of the west that prided itself on outproducing any other place on earth in, hell, sheepshit if you wanted to make a *contest* outten it.

Stringer thought it more prudent to unbuckle his gun rig and stow it, with his Army Issue S&W in a saddlebag under his slicker before he rode any closer to any part-time soldiers packing more serious Army Issue. He was glad he had when, riding around a barn-sized boulder, he came face to face with General Bell's ferocious notion of a road block.

They had a hard rubber tired motor truck parked to either side of the Gold Camp Road, each with headlamps facing south and rear bumpers aimed upslope at him. Neither was as impressive as the boiler plate gun turret mounted on each truck's bed. Just in case the .30-30 machine guns peeking out of the turrets failed to stop any bearded anarchist loping down the wagon trace with an infernal device, they'd strung concertina loops of barbed wire across the right-of-way between the armored trucks. But the pudgy young guardsman wearing glasses and a slung Krag rifle looked less worried as Stringer dismounted up the trail a piece and approached on foot, leading the bay with one hand and holding out old T.S. Murdstone's pass with the other. This was going to be one hell of a time to discover the puffed-up Murdstone was on General Bell's shitlist.

Apparently he wasn't. The summer soldier barely glanced at the familiar printed form before he hauled enough wire out of the way for Stringer to lead the pony through. When a ghostly voice called out from the nearest tin turret, the kid called back, "He's with the M.O.A., Sarge. The C.O. said it was only the *union* guns we had to worry about, remember?"

Stringer felt no call to correct anyone as he remounted

and rode on down the wagon trace. The scenery got more chewed up before he started passing outlying log cabins nobody could even think about building amid such stark surroundings these days. The kitchen match reek of ore refineries hung in the air now. His pony didn't seem to like that, much. Stringer steadied his mount and told it in a soothing tone, "Just be grateful they don't refine *copper* in these parts, you delicate critter. Roasting telluride may not smell of lavender, but it's perfume, next to copper sulfide ore. *Those* fumes will take the hair off a man's chest without unbuttoning his shirt!"

They began to pass more impressive architecture, none moreso than the roofed-over mine machinery running up the slopes to either side. For human beings could always throw another blanket on the bunk or shove some more coal in their cabin stove during the winter months up here. But conveyors, crushers and such needed real protection from the elements if they were to keep producing, and around the clock production was the way anyone but a lawyer made money on a gold mine.

There were, Stringer already knew, more than five thousand shafts producing everything from High Grade to Hot Air in the Cripple Creek field. In the banner year of 1901, those various mines had produced between them, a little over twenty-five million dollars worth of bullion, which sounded like a lot until one divvied the pot between a good sized gang of owners and the forty thousand lesser lights who dug the gold or, with much less effort, from the ones who did the hard work underground at circa three dollars per diem.

The original business center of Cripple Creek had burned to the ground in '96 when a coal oil lamp had taken an unfortunate punch during a punch-out between a barkeep and a whore in the Central Dance Hall. Ten buildings had been left standing after the fire had spread to the dynamite and flammable whiskey in Harder's

General Store, although some blamed part of the horrendous explosion on the boilers of the all-frame and all-steam-heat Palace Hotel betwixt the dance hall and dynamite. So the downtown Stringer rode into that afternoon had been rebuilt of brick and brownstone, albeit in a less flamboyant style than the incinerated Victorian Gingerbread old-timers still recalled so wistfully.

After such a long ride, the first chore Stringer faced, of course, was seeing to the creature comforts of his tired mount. Once he had the bay rubbed down, watered and fed at the livery across from the new brick Palace, he thoughtfully removed his gun rig from the saddle that seemed safe enough in the tack room, for now, and strapped it on before striding up the street to the offices of the *Cripple Creek Crusher*, one of the two reliable newspapers Sam Barca had known of in town. Stringer had no call to suspect the rival *Cripple Creek Prospector* of skullduggery, but as he told the old-timer who came out from the back to study him morosely, Sam Barca had said to look up his old pal, Jeff Keller, at the *Crusher*.

Stringer could see how his crusty boss and this old fart might have gotten to be pals in their cub reporting days. Good Old Jeff just growled, "You sure picked a swell time to pester me. You ever stick type?" to which Stringer replied with a shrug, "Some. I just told you I was a newspaperman." So the older example of the species snorted something about Stringer looking more like a saddle tramp and led him back to the press room.

There, amid the clatter of a fancy new electric press and the smirks of the two printer's devils feeding it blank newsprint and stacking the results, Jeff nodded curtly at a much more traditional sloping typecase and told Stringer, "If you know the game enough for me to bother with you can stick some pesky personals and tell me what you want at the same time, right?"

Stringer said that sounded reasonable and peeled off his hat and jacket to pick up a typesetter's stick and scan the topmost scrap of notepaper impaled on a spike with others near the upper right-hand corner of the ink-stained wooden case. The older man watched just long enough to see Stringer knew the rudiments of sticking type, then he grumped around to the far side, where a similar typecase sloped the other way with a sort of roof ridge between them below eye level. At first, Stringer didn't ask many questions. Sticking type was a lot like roping calves or riding a bike. It came back to you if you'd ever done it before, but you had to get into the swing of it by paying attention to what you were doing for the first few minutes.

To anyone but a printer, a printer's stick looked a lot more like a shallow tin box. When sticking type, you held it in your left hand if you were right-handed, and reached for the metal type with your free hand. If you were unfortunate enough to be born left-handed you *still* stuck type right-handed, if you wanted to work for ninety-nine out of a hundred printing outfits. Each shallow compartment of the sloping case in front of you contained a heap of the same letters, if the printer's devil who refilled the cases from broken up and re-sorted type knew what was good for him. Each metal letter was, of course, the reverse of the impression it left in ink on contact with the newspaper print. Ergo, as Stringer read the hand scrawled copy to be stuck, he had to insert the type in his stick upside down and backwards. Printers were supposed to be able to read that way as well and while it was an old print shop saw, Watch your Ps and Qs! didn't really apply to anyone with a lick of sense. While it was true that a metal type-face reading lower case p would print as q on paper, there were grooves on the slivers of type that warned one at a glance or quick feel when type had been stuck wrong. So it was simply a matter of taking his time and paying attention to the personal notice he was sticking at the moment. The older hand facing him wasn't able to hold out as long. He grudgingly asked how Old Sam Barca was these days and added that Stringer's trip all the way from Frisco proved the dumb Dago still didn't know a mouse in the dark from an all-out assault by Jack The Ripper. When Stringer removed the print order slip he'd just stuck from the spike and proceeded to set a second, mildly asking what they might be jawing about, the local newspaperman said, "All this bull about another big shoot-out up here in the gold fields, of course. I covered the one we had back in the not-really-all-that-gay nineties. Those of us as had families to feed called it a mighty mean business depression. The panic pushed the price of gold down. It was a mighty dumb time to strike for higher wages, but the so-calt Knights of Labor called one. So miners walked out of the shafts all over Colorado, the poor saps."

Stringer double-checked the spelling of the name of the lady who's husband would no longer be responsible for her debts before he told the older newspaperman, "I think I was on my way to Cuba with Teddy and his Rough Riders about that time. The Colorado Guard got to shoot at least as many strikers as Teddy did Spaniards, right?"

Jeff growled, "Don't talk like a damned Democrat. It was in '96, two years afore the war with Spain, the Knights Of Labor declared war on Colorado Capitalism. They failed at Aspen and Leadville. Men with wives and kids to feed don't cotton much to risking their jobs to prove old Karl Marx right. You can't have much of a strike when only a handful of single and no-doubt lazy malcontents refuse to work."

Stringer stuck the last of a line, placed a slug in for some space and began a new one, working faster, now, as he insisted, "Come on, Jeff. I said I never covered the big Cripple Creek strike of the nineties. I never said I heard it was a snowball fight. Sam Barca tells me considerable blood was spilt on both sides, and that you boys here at the Crusher were as sympathetic to the strikers as any paper in Colorado.''

Jeff Keller grimaced and replied, ''What can I tell you? I was still laboring under the impression that this world might be run on the level. Some of the mine owners did try to take advantage of the financial panic by cutting wages. A vainglorious sheriff who looked and talked like Wild Bill, but doubtless sat down to pee, thundered war talk that only encouraged hot heads on the other side to study war. Meanwhile old Winfield Scott Stratton, about as decent a mine owner as ever drew breath at this altitude, signed a contract with John Calderwood, founder of the more reasonable Western Federation Of Miners, for two bits more a shift with the same pay for shorter night shifts.''

Stringer frowned and said, ''Hold on, Jeff. We've been told the W.F.M. is a radical red flag outfit, run by Big Bill Heywood and some like-minded anarchists.''

Jeff Keller locked the stick he'd been filling, picked up another, and growled, ''History could be repeating herself, although things ain't half as bad now as they were then. Calderwood enlisted about eight hundred miners in his then-new union, struck some of the mines owned by more stubborn gents, and then sort of foolishly went down to the flatlands on other union beeswax. He had his fool self two younger and less cool-headed lieutenants, Junius Johnson and Jack Smith, who liked to be called General Smith. Calderwood had no sooner left town than brawling broke out betwixt strikers, and scabs brung in against the very advice of this newspaper and the Colorado Guard. So Johnson and Smith built a half-ass fort atop Bull Hill and both sides commenced lobbing lead and dynamite until it's a pure wonder only a handful were killed outright in the end.''

''The military crushed the uprising, right?'' asked Stringer, only to be told, ''So union handbills and the socialist newspapers printed back east would have it said, only I was here, and that ain't the way it happened. General Tarsney, in command of the troops at the time, was an officer and a gentleman who knew what both words meant. He and his troops busted up fights and policed the goldfields with as even a hands as anyone but a mine owner or a striker might want. So naturally both sides accused the troopers of siding with the other."

"How *did* it end, then?" asked Stringer, really curious now, as he'd always thought the accounts he'd read about the big Colorado mining strikes had been unbiased.

Jeff Keller told him, "The union brought in profcssional toughs. The mine owners did the same, and they had more money to spend that way. The strikers were headquartered over in Altman, around the first mines they'd struck. A hundred and twenty-five company guns caught the Florence and Cripple Creek Railroad over yonder one bright morning. As they were rolling off the flat cars, loaded for bear, a mighty dynamite blast blew the shaft house of the Strong Mine a good five hundred feet in the air. More dynamite went off all about, showering pullies, cables and shattered timber down on the hired guns, who no-doubt reasonably retreated, chased all the way into this town, or Victor, with the union toughs in hot pursuit."

Stringer frowned thoughtfully and demanded, "You say that's how the strike was *broken*, Jeff?" to have the old timer explain, "Sure I do. Johnson and Smith led let's say seven hundred hotheads into town to bust it up. Some of them got busted up in the process, but they mostly made folks *mad* at 'em. Up until they took to knocking down old men and lifting young gal's skirts right here in town, a good many local folk had been rooting for them to win again the stuck-up mine owners. But once the damn-fool union toughs declared war on society in general, well, there were at least fifty thousand souls in this county alone, including a heap of other mining men, who had more use for law and order than any damn notions of Karl Marx or even William Jennings Bryan! This paper, for one, switched positions on the union's demands. The National Guard had to round up the ring leaders, even though General Tarsney didn't think much of the state government we had at the time. Old W.S. Stratton, who'd been as easy to get along with as the union could have hoped for, took the lead in cracking down with a neat divide-and-conquer ploy. He got all the mine owners to go along with three dollars a shift for an eight hour shift, provided all so-called troublemakers on both sides, including their leader Calderwood, stood trial for all the trouble they'd caused."

Stringer whistled softly and said, "I was wondering how Big Bill Heywood got to be the boss of the W.F.M." But Keller told him, "Don't leap to conclusions like an infernal cub. I told you both old Stratton and General Tarsney were smart as well as decent gents. Calderwood and most of the boys on both sides were let off with warnings. Only the rascals who'd actually set off dynamite really got to go to jail. But that was only providing they cease and desist from further shit in and about the Sacred Soil of Colorado. General Smith didn't seem to savvy the terms. He was gunned over in Altman whilst trying to organize another strike. Some say his killer was a company man while others say it was personal. Nobody ever stood trial for the shooting. Old Johnson joined up for the war with Spain and never came back. Old Calderwood was making a more honest, or at least less hectic, living as an assayer, last we heard of him. We know how to handle such assholes, here in Cripple Creek."

Stringer slugged another line before he demanded, "What am I here for, today, in that case? Heywood's taken over the remnants of the W.F.M. to demand a rematch with your Stratton and . . ."

"Stratton's dead." Keller cut in, bleakly, but sounding a mite more cheerful as he continued, "W.S. died in, let's see, 1902 if memory serves me rightly. Lord, what a funeral that was, down to Evergreen Cemetery, in The Springs. But the Mine Owner's Association he ran so swell lives after him, stronger than ever and, thanks to Stratton's clever leadership when leadership was needed, *smarter* than ever. As for Big Bad Bill, the Wild Desperado of the Colorado mine fields, he's only the executive secretary of the W.F.M.; Charles Moyer, a more reasonable cuss, is the president elected by the rank and file. Moyer's only interested in wages and working conditions, like most of the miners, if the truth would be known. Bill Heywood's just a windbag who reads too much. Bert Carlton's issued standing orders on Big Bill. He's likely to experience the joys of tar and feathering if he opens his big mouth in Cripple Creek again!"

Stringer cocked an eyebrow and said, "That's likely why he's been lurking in a back room down at Colorado Springs, then. Who's Bert Carlton, and has anyone told you Harry Orchard's just shown up?"

Jeff Keller shot Stringer a keen look across the ridgepole between them as he replied, "The hell you say! Harry Orchard west of the Big Muddy could mean Moyer's not keeping as tight a rein on his socialist second in command as I would. Bert Carlton is the mine owner who took over the M.O.A. after Stratton died."

"Is he as smart and fair-minded as their original leader?" asked Stringer, noting he'd about finished the backed-up personal ads as Keller answered, "Nobody'll ever beat Stratton at being fair-minded. He come from humble beginnings, as a carpenter up Leadville way, and never lost touch with the working stiffs he grew up among. He left a swell home for orphans and elderly poor folk, down to The Springs, and when Silver Dollar Tabor died, he tore up the promissory notes for the loans he'd made his old boss and old pal after things went sour on Silver Dollar. They say Stratton made sure Tabor's widow, Baby Doe, got to keep their last Leadville mine, the Matchless, and that . . ."

"Never mind ancient history," Stringer cut in, adding, "Tell me what we can expect from the sweet old gent's replacement, Bert Carlton."

Keller thought before he answered, "Firm but fair in his own hard rock way, I reckon. There were some as said old W.S. was too prone to forgive and forget. But whether young Bert goes along in the end, with some of the more reasonable demands, or just hangs tough and busts the W.F.M. a second time, you and Sam Barca are still making elephants outten pack rats."

Stringer insisted, "Damn it, Jeff, the union's already struck most of the mines up here in these hills, hasn't it?" To which the older man replied with a chuckle, "You mean you just noticed? Of course the damn-fool W.F.M. has *called* a strike, and I'd say at least fifty mines betwixt here and say Colorado City are having some trouble getting their ore out of the ground. But Carlton's been recruiting nonunion men as fast or faster than the W.F.M. can march its own off the job. Few of the skilled workers have ever joined the W.F.M. to begin with and any damned hobo can muck ore, and be glad to do so, for three dollars a day."

As Stringer waved the last copy he'd set between them, the older man said, grudgingly, "Not bad, for a big shot newspaperman used to fancy linotype machines and such. It must be Sam Barca who's the asshole. The strike's been on for months and I defy anyone to *notice* it outside, when the boys change shifts any minute, now. The union found out the last time that they can't put the owners out of business with any half-ass strike, and as for trying to *blast* them out a second time, I'd say that was just what Bert Carlton and the more hardcased mine owners are praying for. So far, there's only been one bad accident, earlier this year at the Vindicator Mine, and nobody can prove Harry Orchard had a delicate hand in it. A couple of pit bosses got killed on the seventh level and some say our Harry had been seen in the neighborhood a few hours earlier. But if it was Orchard, he's losing his touch of late. Two dozen nonunion workers scabbing for the M.O.A. came through unscathed when some dynamite went off down yonder, by accident or not."

Stringer shrugged and decided, "Gents like Harry Orchard or even Tom Horn wouldn't get away with half as many killings if proving suspicion was easy. Do you know another unpleasant cuss called T.S. Murdstone, more likely on the other side? I'm supposed to look him up here in Cripple Creek sooner or later."

Jeff Keller, who so far seemed an honest man, swore softly and said, "Make it later. You don't want anything to do with T.S. Murdstone, Stringer. He's a gambling man who won himself a gold mine as well as a heap of enemies in his time. So stay the hell away from him. That way neither he, nor the sore losers gunning for him, are apt to nail you in their crossfire, see?"

CHAPTER SIX

Armed with more savvy on the local situation, Stringer headed for the nearest Western Union office to bring his feature editor up to date and ask if his paper's morgue had any background poop on the people he'd heard of so far. Cripple Creek had a serious central business district for its population figures because a lot of its population was engaged in serious business. So the once tiny and still rustic mining and refining community was served by three railroads, along with a surprisingly up to date interurban trolly car system that ran on electricity as well as narrow gauge as far as Independence. But most of the downtown business establishments seemed to be saloons, with or without hot and cold running hostesses, and Stringer had to ask directions to the telegraph office near the central depot.

As he spied the black and yellow sign he was seeking down the road a piece, Stringer noticed white duck military tents, a lot of military tents, pitched cheek by jowl in a good-sized vacant lot across from the railroad depot. He passed the depot and Western Union for a look-see up the slopes across the railroad yards and, sure enough, there was an even bigger herd of tents up that way, with a battery of mountain howitzers holding the higher ground and dominating, if not outright threatening Saloon Row. So whether General Sherman Bell was as fair-minded as the guard commander who'd put down the last trouble or not, he sure seemed to know his job, for a part-time man-of-destiny.

As Stringer retraced his steps to the telegraph office, he spied a couple of troopers holding up a wall across the way with their backs. It wasn't clear whether they were just lounging there or keeping an eye on the strategic telegraph office. They both had their bayonets fixed to their casually slung Krags. So Stringer suspected their sergeant of the guard had told them they were free to stand at ease, perhaps *ordered* to stand at ease, and keep their first and seventh general orders in mind.

The seventh general order any sentry was supposed to remember forbade idle conversation with curious civilian males or good-looking females passing by one's post. The *first* general order was, of course, to keep an eye peeled and report any and everything one might notice on or about one's post to the corporal of the guard every time he came by, which was at least once an hour if those boys were half as sneaky-slick as Stringer was commencing to suspect.

He didn't care if they reported a man dressed like a cowboy going inside to send a wire or more. Knock wood, the good general hadn't shut down *all* communications with the outside world, yet. But the pretty blond lady clerk inside looked so cheered-up to see a customer, he suspected business had slowed down of late. He said as much, reaching for some yellow telegram forms and hauling out his own stub pencil. She nodded and confided, "The soldiers arrested a customer, right out front, the first day they arrived. Nobody knows why, so it's sort of discouraged casual communications ever since."

He said that sounded grim and asked what the poor cuss had looked like, and what he might have sent by wire that so upset General Sherman Bell. She shrugged and said, "He just looked like a hard rock man to me, dusty work duds and one of those caps they wear. He didn't get to send any wires to anyone. They grabbed him on the walk out front, like I said."

He asked how, in that case, anyone could be certain he'd meant to send wires to begin with. She told him, "Oh, he must have. He had this slip of paper in one hand and the latch of yon door in the other, just as the soldiers grabbed him. They tried to get the paper away from him. Only he stuck it in his mouth and got it down before they could make him spit it out, see?"

Stringer grimaced and said, "I do, now. They must have a black list. I'm glad I'm not on it. I hope."

Then he was too busy writing to jaw with her for a time, pretty as she might have been. When he'd finished he told her, "I'd like to send this collect. We'd still best send it as a night letter. My boss weeps bitter tears just thinking about day rates and gives me a hard time every time I waste a nickel, he says, on a word we might have gotten by without."

She dimpled across the counter at him and said she understood as she scanned the two-page message, moving her pink lips as she silently counted, and added, "You do have a lot to say about those silly old socialists, don't you? I hope you understand this won't go out until late tonight, after all the day-rate messages have been sent?"

He nodded and told her, "I'd have sent it day-rates if I hadn't learned at my sweet old feature editor's knee that night letters were way cheaper and still beat the U.S. Mails. How come you call the W.F.M. socialist? It was my understanding they were just a mine worker's union."

She wrinkled her pert nose and answered, "I guess my dear old daddy and two grown brothers know the difference betwixt an honest workman's guild and a passle of red-flag troublemakers with un-American notions about private property. My dear old daddy is a shift foreman at the Plymouth Rock, up on Ironclad Hill, and both my brothers draw top wages at the Buena Vista."

Stringer asked her, dryly, "I take it none of the men in your family are interested in joining the W.F.M. then?" To which she replied with a firm nod, "You take it right, sir. My daddy did join the Knights Of Labor, he says, in a moment of madness no doubt inspired by good will to man and forty-rod whisky. But he says all he gained from the experience was the wisdom to say no to future flimflam men calling their fool selves union organisers. My dear old daddy never got a thing but trouble for the union dues he paid the infernal Knights of Labor. They promised him and the others more pay for shorter hours and, in the end, all they wound up with was a blacklisting by the mine owners."

"Yet he wound up a shift foreman in the end?" asked Stringer with a politely raised eyebrow.

She told him, "We got off awfully lucky. The late and sincerely lamented W.S. Stratton owned all the mines on Ironclad Hill and he was a dear forgiving boss, once he and the other mine owners had busted the big strike and deported the ring leaders from the state. Some of the other big shots wanted to blacklist all the workers who'd even paid for a fool union card, the Pinks had copied down all the membership lists, of course. But Mister Stratton allowed it was dumb to fire good workers who hadn't done anything wicked and may have learned a good lesson. So my dear old daddy and his friends stayed on, and proved their decent boss right."

She looked as if she was fixing to blubber up about it as she added, "When dear old W.S. sold his mine holdings and retired back in '99, he made sure the new owners, an English mining company, would keep the workers on at the same pay. Me and my whole family went to pay our respects when the sweet old gent died, down to Colorado Springs. That infernal new bunch of organizers won't get very far with any of the old timers here in Cripple Creek, I'll vow!"

He assured her he himself had no intention of joining either the W.F.M. or M.O.A. and then, since the day was about shot and he hadn't made any other plans for that evening, he asked what time she got off, and whether she had anyone to escort her home during the current state of martial law. She dimpled at him some more and told him she got off at six. Then she added demurely that her fiance, a blaster working the lobster shift at the Findlay Mine in Independence, would arrive in plenty of time to escort her home, thanks to the swell electric trolley line they'd provided to shrink the gold fields down to size for courting couples.

So he could only wish her and her hard rock boyfriend well and content himself with the silent observation that nobody got to win 'em all.

As he sashayed out he attempted to console himself with the further observation that making love to pretty gals would just be another chore, like paying one's bills, if a man knew he was stuck with kissing *all* of 'em he met up with.

It didn't work. That blonde inside had been pretty and well-built and he was simply too young and healthy to consider retiring from the sport just yet. At the rate he was going, he figured to wind up a dirty old man. Or at least he sure hoped so.

Then, in the lengthening shadows outside, he was forced to reconsider the odds on his reaching old age or even his next birthday, when a tough-looking bozo dressed halfway cowboy and halfway preacher, or undertaker, stepped away from the wall planks he'd been lounging against to softly growl, "Might you be that newspaperboy, MacKail, little darling?"

Stringer regarded the heavy-set and blue-jawed stranger thoughtfully as he considered whether to answer before or after he went for his own six-gun. For the burly brute wore *two*, cross-draw but low and tied down, under his open frock coat. A tied down holster gave a shootist some advantage in a leather-slapping contest, it was said, but Stringer had always avoided such sinister trimmings for more than one good reason.

To begin with, a tied down holster only gave its wearer an edge when he was walking at a finite target in a preplanned space. It could mess up your draw if you had to draw sudden sitting down or, worse yet, mounted up. But the greatest disadvantage to swaggering about in a tie down rig was that almost everyone you swaggered at knew, as was the case right now, they were facing a cuss who was either damned foolish or damned serious, which sometimes added up to the same thing.

Stringer decided any man who'd call another man little darling, knowing he was packing a gun of his own, had to be at least as dumb as he might be dangerous, so he answered just as sweetly, "You can call me anything but late for breakfast, *sweetheart*. What's it to you?"

Stringer was braced for most any move but the next one. The mean-looking cuss suddenly spun on one high heel and walked off suddenly, whipping around the corner of the building to vanish from human ken, or at least Stringer's.

The object of the sinister stranger's recent scrutiny stared up the walk at nothing much, muttering, "I give up. What in thunder was *that* all about?" when he heard boot heels on the walk behind him and, while it hardly seemed possible anyone could have circled a whole building *that* fast, he still felt a certain tingling up the back of his neck as he whirled to get his spine to the wall and his gun hand even closer to his .38. But he was glad he hadn't actually filled his fist when he saw it was one of the state troopers from across the way, striding in step with an older and fatter cuss with corporal's stripes on his blue sleeves.

As Stringer nodded at them, with a bemused expression, the dumpy part-time corporal stared back just as bemused to ask, "Did we bust up a fight or a budding romance just now, cowboy?"

Stringer smiled more broadly to reply, "That jasper didn't hang about long enough to say, thanks to you boys. I see that when your General Bell declared martial law in these parts he wasn't whistling Dixie!"

The corporal of the guard shrugged and told him, "Governor Peabody declared martial law. Our job is to see nobody fucks up in this here part of Colorado. Do you have a permit to pack that there pistol, cowboy?"

Stringer nodded hopefully and told them both, "I'm neither a cowhand nor a danger to the community and you'll kindly note my hands are nowhere near my sidearm as I attempt to produce some documentation for my lawful presence in these parts."

Neither made any move to shoot Stringer as he got out his press credentials, California gun permit and the military pass old Murdstone had bestowed upon him. He handed all three to the corporal, who looked them over with one eyebrow cocked before he announced, "Your out-of-state license to pack sidearms don't mean shit in Colorado, and it was my understanding neither our civil, nor military leaders wanted this anarchist unrest glorified in any damned newspapers."

"How do you feel about that military pass?" asked Stringer, reaching for straws but trying not to let it show. It must not have. The guard corporal handed all the paper back to him, growling, "Ours is not to reason why. I don't know the officer as signed your pass, but it looks like our own stationary, so I reckon you're free to carry on unless or until you get some higher up the totem pole than *us* pissed off at you. Let's get back to that other cuss with two guns, and no permit to carry either, as far as we could see just now."

Stringer answered, honestly, "Your guess is as good as mine. I never saw the asshole before."

"Then how come you call him an asshole?" asked the corporal with a frown that indicated he might have a smarter job in civilian life.

Stringer explained, "You boys guessed right about him acting sort of odd and I thank you for busting it up before it got downright surly. I can't say what he wanted. But I feel safe in calling him an asshole because he knew me by name, meaning he knew me by rep, and still telegraphed his intent to give me some damned sort of hard time when you two could see, from clean across the street, I was wearing this hardware of my own."

The dumpy noncom favored Stringer with a thoughtful once-over before he decided, "I don't know your rep, but unless you're known as a mighty weak sister, I follows your drift. Do you want to press charges against that two-gun boogyman, if we see him again?"

Stringer thought, shook his head, and said, "I would if I had a thing on him that I might get a judge and jury to buy. But thanks to you boys, he lit out before we got down to just how sore we might or might not be about what. You'd know, of course, if he was a Pinkerton man trying to help your superiors keep a lid on the story up here in these hills?"

The corporal didn't go the least bit shifty-eyed as he shook his head and told Stringer, "Nobody's told us anything about any Pinks working for or against us in these parts. If there are any secret agents working on our side, the way that old boy just acted was all wrong. When the Pinks went after the Molly Maguires back in '75 they never acted beligerent on the streets. They infiltrated the secret society and just collected evidence 'til they had enough to hang two dozen or so of the anarchists."

Stringer knew better than to ask a member of the Colorado National Guard why anyone who wanted to start or join a mine union had to be an anarchist. He settled for saying, "The Molly Maguire trouble was a mite before my time. But your point's well taken that a professional sneak tends to behave more sneaky than that surly son of a bitch just acted. I reckon I'll just have to ask him next time we meet, and it'll be up to the judge and jury to decide whether the winner was in the right or wrong."

The corporal said, "Don't bet on that, MacKail. For openers, the only criminal courts in operation up this way, until further notice, are courts martial. General Bell don't hold with juries or, come to study on it, any formal proceedings worth mention. Under the rules of martial law, the constitutional requirements of a speedy trial don't apply. So why bother? You get your ass busted in or about Cripple Creek, Feather Merchant, and you can figure on suffering Durance Vile until the emergency is over, or until General Bell gets good and ready to court martial you or cut you loose, see?"

Stringer grimaced and replied, "I do, now. Remind me not to get myself arrested by you boys as I wend my weary way through this neck of the woods."

The corporal of the guard smiled pleasantly enough, as he warned Stringer, "I thought I just did, MacKail."

CHAPTER SEVEN

Sunsets were tricky in the Colorado high country. For, while the late afternoon sun had soaring crags to hide its fool self behind, it was still high enough above the true horizon to bestow a long lavender, crimson and burnt orange gloaming as, all up and down the rolling gold fields, mine whistles announced it was time to come to work or go home to supper. Men working the day shift could go years without ever seeing broad daylight. Yet, it was the boys who worked the suppertime to midnight shift who demanded and usually got that extra two to six bits. For unless they were married, and happily at that, they missed a heap of the pleasures Cripple Creek had to offer after dark.

Stringer was regarding some of them with mild interests as he lounged against one end of the bar in the Cousin Jack Saloon. He'd long since booked himself a single at the nearby and now-fireproof Palace Hotel. He'd eaten some chili con carne under fried eggs, followed by coffee and cake, so now all he had to worry about was getting tired enough to turn in, alone.

He knew an overnight or even a week-end stranger in a mining town infested mostly with hard-up males was no place to scout for True Romance and he'd always been just too romantic-natured to pay for it. The two gals dancing on the small but lit-up stage at the far end of the bar made it easier for him to consider a night of celibacy. While the cancan they were canning to a merry but off-key ragtime tune was no doubt meant to inspire the male libido, one of the dancing gals was too skinny, the other was too fat, and both were about as kissable as the north end of a pig headed south. As their dance got dirtier Stringer felt even more depressed and shifted his gaze out the grimy plate glass he stood closer to. He didn't see anyone out yonder he wanted to kiss any harder, but at least none of the mining men made him taste that recent chili as they strode by with their lunch and toolboxes, some more tired looking than others, but nobody looking downright pissed.

Unlike the coal miners just to the south, around Florence and on down to Trinidad, the hard-rock miners of the Cripple Creek area looked about as clean coming up out of the mountains as they had going down into them eight or more hours before. Telluride ore was tough to bust and sharp as busted glass to work with, but the work was still cleaner in a hard rock mine and most hard rock men felt a cut above coal miners, who tended to get killed even more often for even lower wages. None of the gold miners passing by looked fresh as petunias, of course. The temperature rose as the shafts went down and there was no way to sweat that hard without the gray dust sticking some. But he knew they'd look clean enough at the supper table after no more than a quick shower or, hell, a good splashing over the wash basin out back, and what the hell, they were making three times as much as an average ranch hand and few ranch hands would allow a miner worked harder. So Stringer wasn't too surprised to see the main streets so lightly guarded despite all the roughly-clad mining men striding up or down it at the moment. He *had* seen troopers, plenty of them, positioned more cleverly than obviously on strategic corners and even sandbagged rooftops as he'd prowled about, some, after his odd run-in just outside the telegraph office. But despite that noncom's dire remarks about martial law, or even the posters saying much the same thing from many a Cripple Creek wall, neither the workers out yonder nor the other patrons of this particular saloon seemed to notice or care that the town had a heap of Krag rifles and even heavier weapons trained on it.

He'd found it impossible to strike up an interesting conversation about the strike that was supposed to be raging in the gold fields at the moment, either here at the Cousin Jack, or earlier at the chili parlor. Everyone he'd asked had either said his particular mine hadn't been struck, that he didn't work in any infernal gold mine, or that it was none of Stringer's beeswax *where* he worked or how he might feel about such bullshit. Stringer assumed those old boys likely knew a mite more about the trouble, if there was going to *be* any trouble. So far, the news tips about blood and slaughter in and about the gold fields hadn't panned out any more exciting than Jack London's tip about mad scientists blowing out fuses in the flatter country to the east with semidomesticated lightning bolts. That was the trouble with news tips. There was often little or nothing to them and when there *was* some basis for the tip it tended to pan out, in the end, that rumors of a dray of watermelons overturning had been based on someone dropping a jar of olives. Poor old Jack and even Vania the Russian agent, bless her overactive ass and imagination, had been led down the garden path by little more than butter-fingered wiring, and the clumsy attempts of drunks or tyros to cover up their mistakes without really knowing what they were supposed to be doing.

The big emergency here in Cripple Creek seemed to be turning out even dumber, inspired by little more than half-ass labor agitation and memories of that earlier, more violent strike. Now that he'd been on the scene for a while, it seemed hardly anyone wanted any part of the radical W.F.M. and, even if half the miners had signed up with the union, the mine owners still seemed to hold all the high cards in the game this time, as they'd had the last. It was small wonder Big Bill Heywood and even the sinister Harry Orchard were forced to do their plotting miles away in Colorado Springs. There was hardly any way to get anywhere near the mining area without military permission, and if the Pinkertons hadn't furnished the mine owners and military with the names and descriptions of all the important union organisers by now, the Pinkertons hadn't been earning their usual handsome fee for such activity. After all, the agency had been founded by the same old sneak who'd organized the U.S. Secret Service for Lincoln during a time of far more serious strife.

Stringer was sorely tempted to just chuck it in and head back to Frisco via The Springs, where good old Vania still might like him just as much. The tale of Nikola Tesla inventing a better wireless telegraph system for the Czar Of All The Russians had Sam Barca's notion of strikers and strike breakers lobbing dynamite at one another beat all hollow. But at the rate things were going, neither lead was going to result in even a Sunday Supplement feature and, hell, he was *encouraged* to lie like a rug for the Sunday Supplement.

These days, old Jack London hardly wrote for anything else and he sure got a lot of mileage out of warning the white race of the yellow peril and the days to come when wars would be fought in the sky by daredevils in flying machines. Old Jack's tales of impending doom were a caution. But, meanwhile, an honest newspaperman was supposed to either file the truth or admit he had no infernal story worth printing.

He finished the last of his beer and turned his back on the dirty but ugly cancan dancers. There had to be something more interesting to do, even in Cripple Creek, and he was stuck up here at least until his boss, Sam Barca, agreed with his assessment of the true situation. He knew what Sam would think of a follow-up in the mysterious winking lights down in Colorado Springs, but he figured he'd at least have a word with that Hotwire Hamilton and, of course, old Vania, as he waited for a train back to less confusing parts.

He'd noticed a Nickelodean catty-corner across from that chili joint he'd stopped by earlier. He hoped they'd have some moving pictures he hadn't already seen more than once. But here in the wilds of Colorado, he doubted it. Even on Market Street back in Frisco they kept running the same dumb scenes of railroad locomotives rushing right at you, Little Egypt doing her bumps and grinds right at you, or that singularly unattractive couple kissing, over and over, as if any man, even as ugly as *he* was, could get the least enjoyment out of swapping spit with such a fat and mannish old gal. Stringer had tried to be fair about it, the second time he'd had to sit through it, but in truth the old gal had looked as if she shaved as often as the old bird slobbering at her and he'd been mighty bewildered to learn over the wire service how Anthony Comstock, the moral crusader who'd tried to have the painter of September Morn arrested, had declared that footage a dire threat to the moral fiber of These United States.

He felt sure that was why every Nickelodean in the country kept showing those idiots kissing, as he stepped out into the soft gloaming to head toward the Nickelodean.

He didn't find out that night whether they were offering The Kiss, Little Egypt, or The Great Train Robbery. For he'd barely left the Cousin Jack before a wispy dark phantom fell in beside him in the tricky light to whisper, "There's someone who would like a word with you, Mister MacKail. If you'll but walk this way I'll show you the way, and it's not at all far, you see."

It was a tired joke, but Stringer still had to reply he couldn't walk that way on a bet, since he'd noticed the small stranger's voice was female as well as accented in a delightfully fey way.

Her coal black hair had been swept up more Tumbleweed than Gibson Girl, and her cheap summer shift seemed about the color and texture of tent-worm webbing. But she was a rather pretty little waif and he felt sure she and her pals knew it as she took him by the left elbow and tried to steer him around the next corner, assuring him once more that they didn't have far to go. But Stringer kept going the same damned way as he informed her in a good-natured growl that it had been his great-great-grandad, not himself, who'd gotten off the ship from Glasgow, and added, "The first time a pretty lady I'd never seen before extended me an invite to go roaming in the gloaming into parts unknown, her accent was more Mexican than Welsh and I was just sixteen years old. So *that* time I had some *excuse* for being so dumb."

She murmured something in a lingo Stringer found even harder to fathom than the Gaelic he at least knew how to cuss in and insisted, "It's important, you see! It's the saving of yourself from trouble and not the causing of it we desire, look you!"

He chuckled fondly down at her and answered, "I was big for my age and there were only two of 'em waiting for me and my gringo boots in that back alley, that time. I don't know what I'd have done if that sweet Señorita had set me up for three or more of her kith and kin. So suffice it to say, I vowed then and there that if the Good Lord let me make it to seventeen I'd never act that stupid again."

"Then don't you want to hear our well-meant warning?" She protested as she tried once more, in vain, to steer his bigger and stronger form away from the straight and narrow to his brighter-lit and brick-walled chosen shelter for the night. But his natural nose for news naturally prompted him to tell her, "I'm checked into the Palace. Anyone who wants to talk to me can ask for me at the desk. They have telephones in every room and I'll be proud to come down to the lobby and jaw with anybody about most anything, agreed?"

She sniffed rather grandly for a lady with the scent of boiled cabbage in her hair and demanded, "Do you really think the likes of me and mine would be allowed in the lobby of the grand and glorious Palace of Cripple Creek?" To which he could only reply, "Why not? They let *me* sign in, didn't they? This is America, Taffy. American room clerks are more interested in the color of your dinero than the old school tie you might or might not be wearing. This is a rough and ready mining town, not Saint Lou or Colorado Springs, where all the big shots keep their wives and daughters safe from rude whistles. You tell anyone who wants the loan of my ear that I'll hear 'em out at my hotel, with my back to a brick wall instead of the cold night air. If they don't want to powwow with me under those conditions, well, I'm not so sure I want to meet up with 'em to begin with."

They were now within sight of the well-lit hotel entrance. She didn't tell him whether she was taking his message to anyone or just avoiding the light. One minute she was tagging along and the next one he was striding along alone, so he just kept striding, his back itching under his blue denim jacket until he was in the fern infested lobby and no sore losers had pegged a parting shot at him after all.

As a seasoned traveler, Stringer had naturally hung on to his room key after paying the infernal bellhops for it the first time. So he would have simply gone on up to his single if the desk clerk hadn't called him over to tell him, "They're expecting you in the billiard room, straight back and to the left of that bookcase with the moosehead over it, Mister MacKail."

Stringer frowned and muttered, mostly to himself,

"That was fast. Too fast, as a matter of fact. Who on earth are we talking about, landlord?"

The clerk looked surprised and said, "Mister Murdstone and the others, of course. I thought you knew you were supposed to meet him here this evening."

Stringer smiled thinly and replied, "I do now. I take it old T.S. is a guest here, too, this being the best, if not the only, hotel up here amid the pup tents?"

The clerk sniffed and assured him there were at least a dozen lesser establishments in Cripple Creek, provided one didn't mind coal oil illumination and crapping down the hall. Stringer said he'd heard as much and ambled toward the back of Cripple Creek's answer to Denver's Brown Palace.

Like its namesakes in Denver and Frisco, the Cripple Creek Palace had been wired for electricity as well as fitted out with modern plumbing. Stringer hadn't tested the flush commode in his room upstairs, yet, but he assumed it'd work when and if he pulled the chain. The electric lighting might have been just a mite different if they'd consulted Stringer on interior decoration. Though he'd seen moose heads with orange light bulbs glowing from each and every antler prong before, he'd never developed much of a taste for the sight.

He heard his name being hailed as he circled around to the billiard room, where the light bulbs were whiter and shining down on the green felt from a more natural looking chandelier of mule deer antlers. The cuss who'd called out to him was, naturally, T.S. Murdstone in the ample flesh. Most of the other middle-aged and well-heeled-looking gents were about as portly. They'd peeled off their fancy frock coats to play billiards, as shooting pool was called by such fancy dudes, in their shirtsleeves, brocaded vests and diamond stick pins. When Murdstone invited Stringer to join the game, he hauled off his rough rider hat to show he might be staying a spell, but allowed he'd just watch until he figured out how you shot pool without any pockets for the infernal balls to drop into.

As Murdstone introduced him all around, Stringer shook friendly but didn't recall whose face went with which name, for the most part. There were almost a dozen and most of them didn't seem all that impressed with Stringer, either. He perked up when he was introduced to Bert Carlton, having heard the name not all that long before. The new ramrod of the Mine Owner's Association didn't look or talk all that tough, but there was a quiet firmness to both his handshake and the set of his jaw that made Stringer glad he hadn't come up here to shut down any of old Bert's mines.

He perked up even more when he was introduced to the older and more reckless looking J.H. Hammond, asking, "Aren't you the mining magnate who, a few years ago, backed Nikola Tesla's experiments with man-made lightning?"

Hammond looked more sheepish than famous as he replied. "I'm more a mining engineer than a magnate. I just show the boys how to get the rock out and refined. They're welcome to the financial anguish of staking and proving claim one. As to that lunatic, Tesla, my lawyer and my oldest boy, John Junior, got me into that fiasco. Both me and old George Westinghouse had used Lenny Curtis as a patent attorney. Lawyer Curtis is good at that and holds an interest in the Colorado Springs Electric Company."

When Stringer asked if Hammond's lawyer was connected with the power company here in Cripple Creek, the older man shrugged and told him, "I neither know nor care. I can tell you the juice works better up this way thanks to those experiments they never recovered from, than down by The Springs. My son, John Junior, met Tesla through our mutual lawyer. Curtis has filed more patents in Tesla's name than one can shake a stick at. My boy knows more about electricity than me. Or at least he's more interested in the subject. Betwixt him and Curtis, I was talked into persuading my friends on the county board into letting the maniac set up shop in that cow pasture, gratis. Lenny Curtis talked his own pals at the Electric Company into providing power for Old Nick's experiments, all he needed, free."

T.S. Murdstone butted in with, "Never mind that long-gone and crazy Croatian. It's time to settle who's betting for or against my young pal, here."

Stringer blinked in confusion and demanded, "Hold on, T.S. Who said anything about my betting anything? I just told you I don't know much about shooting pool without pockets."

Murdstone laughed sort of satanic and replied, "Hell, old son, I told the boys you were fixing to drive my Panard all the way up to Summit Lodge, atop Pikes Peak, and more than one man here has as much as told me I was full of shit."

Stringer chuckled wryly and said, "That sounds fair, T.S. I don't recall bragging that outrageously about my ability to ride any tin buckboard half so high up any hill at all!"

Hammond wasn't the only gent there who smiled at the florid-faced Murdstone mighty knowingly. The gambling man led Stringer by one arm to the corner bar, ordering them both forty-rod boilermakers as he almost hissed at Stringer, "Damn it, you can't let me down at this late date! I thought we had us a deal, MacKail!"

Stringer shrugged and said, "We did. You wrote out that military pass for me and to my surprise the troopers took you serious as you seem to take yourself. But if you'll think back, I only agreed to adjust your damn-fool carburetor and spark for you. I never agreed to be your fool *jockey,* if that's what you call a kid who races motor cars. I'm here on my own serious business, T.S. Can't you drive your own damn Panard up the peak, seeing how fast you like to drive it everywhere else?"

He meant that as reasonable as he thought it sounded. But the dumpy Murdstone still stared up at him about the way Caesar must have stared that time at old Brutus, groaning, "I'm afraid of heights. Even if I wasn't, that infernal Dutch Ritter has a driver for his own blue Buick that can't weigh a hundred and twenty pounds while I, as you may have noticed, just happen to be a man of parts."

Stringer had to laugh as the barkeep served their heroic drinks. Forty-rod whiskey wasn't a brand, it was decent liquor, safe to drink at over a hundred proof and hence apt to drop you on your ass before you could walk forty rods after putting down, or dropping, the shotglass. At the altitude of Cripple Creek most men could get mighty smashed on ale or porter. But Stringer had one sneaky advantage over most mortal drinkers. Hailing from a truculent highland clan, no matter how far removed from the auld glens, he'd been taught to sip the pure malt creature from childhood, or at least on family occasions, when the wee ones were neither left out nor allowed to fall down just because they were unconscious. So he knew that if Murdstone was trying to get him drunk enough to go along with such foolishness, Murdstone was wasting his jingle, as well as putting himself in danger of falling down faster.

It was good stuff, though, and Stringer said so as he sipped it, neat, ignoring the stunned expression on the fat boy's florid face.

So that would have been that, had not they been joined about then by an even fatter old fart Stringer recalled on their second intro as the one they called Dutch Ritter. Ritter was a mining magnate and let everyone know how rich he was, right off. He favored them both with the same knowing grin and asked, "What's the matter, T.S., has your jockey turned into a chicken on you?"

Stringer cocked an eyebrow as he carefully put his glass back on the bar, softly saying, "It's not a matter of white feathers sticking out of anyone, Mister Ritter. I'd be proud to race your Buick up the mountain, if I was twelve years old and had nothing better to do. But you see, I don't work for Mister Murdstone, here, or come to study on it, *you*, either. My own boss sent me here to cover the big mining strike, if only I could find one going on."

Ritter shrugged and said, "Oh, all my mines have been struck by the W.F.M. They've been out even longer at Bert Carlton's shafts down the trollyway at Independence. But you said your paper sent you here to cover *important* stories, MacKail. We're always having labor trouble up here in these hills. But how many races up Pikes Peak have you ever covered?"

Stringer scowled and said, "*Touché*. But you boys sure take it mighty calm when the union shuts you down."

Ritter snorted in disbelief and demanded, "Who said anything about anyone being shut down? As a matter of fact some of us, myself included, are making money on the union's latest blunder. Before my regular crew walked off the job I was stuck with the three dollar a day minimum our association agreed to the last time. Two thirds of the nonunion crew I have working for me now, are content with $2.50 a shift, for few of the scum have ever held such fine jobs."

Stringer asked, without thinking all that hard, when mucking hard rock at wages like that had become such a fine job. Ritter looked innocent as well as smug when he replied, "Since the Lord provided in his wisdom that some men were meant to haul water and hew wood whilst others with the wherewithal to hire help didn't *have* to. You don't even have to advertise to get common laborers up here at such swell day wages. We do have to pay our blasters and such a mite more, but them as toil under the mountain for $2.50 a shift are making over twice the pay of a cowhand, and you can't say cowhands don't get hurt on the job as often."

Stringer frowned thoughtfully and replied, "I don't know which job is more dangerous, but faced with such a grim choice, I reckon I'd rather work cows. For openers you get your room and board as well as a dollar a day to start, off most cattle outfits. But I reckon some gents would rather muck gold ore for more money, so I take back my dumb question and agree you can likely get all the scabs you'll need to break the strike this time as well."

Murdstone clapped Stringer on the back and chortled, "There you go. I told you racing this infernal Dutchman up Pikes Peak was more important than any fool labor problems or even that mad scientist's pet lightning. Do you reckon we ought to run both motor cars over to the cog railroad by flatcar or on their own expensive rubber tires, MacKail?"

Stringer was about to say neither proposition appealed to him when Dutch Ritter horned in to jeer, "Why don't you just pay up like a sport, T.S.? You know you ain't up to driving such a scary road yourself, even if your French machine could haul your big behind that high. As for this newspaper boy in a cowboy suit . . ."

"How much money are we talking about?" Stringer cut in, even as he stared down at his empty shot glass and refrained from asking it how in thunder it had gotten that way. Dutch Ritter told him, "T.S. and me have twenty grand riding on who brakes to a stop in front of the Summit Lodge in front of impartial witnesses. Did you have, say, a side bet in mind, MacKail?"

Stringer nodded soberly and said, "I did. I reckon you don't know me well enough to take my marker, eh?" and he wasn't surprised or even too insulted when Dutch Ritter replied, "All bets are cash in these parts, no offense. But feel free to bet as much as you like on your own or anyone else's ass and I reckon I can cover it."

Stringer started to reach for his wallet, saw he'd only get laughed at if he bragged on that sort of jingle to a herd of mining moguls, and growled, "I haven't been paid for the last couple of stories I've filed from the field.

I've managed to stow away a few more hundred in my bank account. If I wired right now I might be able to scrape up a thousand, all told, if that's not too rich for your blood."

Dutch Ritter was too polite, or too cautious, to laugh right in Stringer's face. He still sounded mighty smug as he replied, "I reckon I can manage that, High Roller. But just what might we be betting on, exactly?"

Stringer said, "I thought it was plain to see. High Rolling, of course. If I brake Mister Murdstone's Panard to a safe stop in front of that lodge atop Pikes Peak, I win. If I fail, you win. What could be fairer than that?"

Dutch Ritter shook his head and answered, "A *race*. Any damned fool can get a motor car to the top of Pikes Peak, if he takes long enough, and for a thousand dollars it might be worth his while to *push* it all the way. Let's say you get there ahead of my motor car and driver, or vice versa, even money, with winner take all?" He was holding out his fat palm as he asked, so Stringer shook on it and once he'd done so, Ritter turned away to head back to the game, announcing, "I think I just picked up a bonus for the kid who'll be driving for me, boys. Anyone else want to get in on the horseless carriage race of the century?"

Stringer turned back to the barkeep and held up two fingers as he muttered, "My turn, T.S. Then I got to run back to Western Union and gather in some sheaves. I sure hope you can stall 'til I can receive and cash some money orders in the cold gray."

Murdstone nodded happily and said, "Don't worry, old son, that cheap bastard's not about to pass on a chance to cover all the bets he can sucker anyone to make. I may just raise the ante my own sweet self, you impetuous youth. To tell you the pure truth, the two of you had me worried there, for a mite. How much do you weigh, afore I get in any deeper with that cheap Dutch bastard and his even money wagers."

Stringer shrugged and said, "I don't climb on the

scales all that often. Last time I had my fortune told, the machine assured me for the same penny that I weighed a tad over one-seventy-five, gun and all. Of course, it assured me I was about to run off to some island paradise with the most beautiful girl in the world and here I am in the middle of the continent and I've yet to meet Miss Ellen Terry or even that artist's model as got Stanford White shot. What difference does it make, anyway?''

Murdstone explained, ''Ritter's machine is spanking new and they say them new Buicks are speedy to start off with. But his motor car by itself ain't what's kept the betting on my machine so modest. They tell me Dutch has stung members of the sporting set before with his big blue Buick and little bitty driver. I fear I got into this over my head before I found out the little squirt who'll be driving up the Pikes Peak wagon trace in place of the big bastard is a well-known prize driver from the other side of The Pond!''

Stringer smiled thinly and replied, ''There's no such thing as a well-known motor car racer, T.S.. I'd have heard if there was. My paper covers all the sporting events as well as all the gold mine strikes. Horseless carriages have been racing horses, locomotives and even each others since the late 1880s, but the results have been too spotty for anyone to get *famous* at it. Can you rig it so's we don't have to race Ritter's driver of international renown this side of, let's say noon, tomorrow?''

Murdstone nodded, thoughtfully, and said, ''I reckon. Most of the boys would as rather board the cog train after noon than *afore* it. For even in summer it takes the sun a spell to heat things comfortable atop Pikes Peak. But are you sure you can drive my Panard all the way up there in half a day?'' To which Stringer could only reply, ''I'm going to have to, unless I aim to lose a heap more dinero than I can afford to.''

CHAPTER EIGHT

When Stringer got back to Western Union, he saw the young blonde behind the counter had been replaced by an old bald bird of his own gender. He didn't ask how come. Anyone could see the street lighting and electric trolly cars out front were working just fine up this way. He'd asked Murdstone not to agree to an early start to their unusual sporting event with the speed of even electrical communications in mind. As he handed his two messages across the counter he told the clerk, "I know that at even a nickel a word there's no way either my banker or paymaster is apt to get even one money order back to me this side of Ten or Eleven A.M. But just in case I get lucky, how early can you boys cash either one?"

The clerk didn't answer until he'd scanned both of Stringer's urgent demands for dinero. Then he whistled and said, "We're talking real money here. No way we could do her outside banking hours. For we don't keep but a hundred or so at a time in our own office safe."

Stringer nodded but said, "I didn't ask you to cash a

money order before one arrives. I asked how soon you could, once it did."

The clerk looked pained and replied, "Look, I only work here, and at night, at that. It'll be up to the day shift to run you over to our bank with a voucher and to tell the truth I'm not sure just how early they'll let you have the money once you get there."

"Don't banks open at nine up here in the hills?" asked Stringer, only to be told, "The banks do. I can't speak for their *vaults*. Thanks to Butch and Sundance, banking's got mighty up-to-date in Colorado of late. They got one of them new time locks over to the bank we keep our own funds in. Unless it's the time of day the branch manager says the vault should be open for customers, neither Sundance nor the Spanish Inquisition could force a teller to open it, see?"

Stringer growled, "I know how time locks work. I don't keep my own money in a coffee can, no matter how beat-up this hat may look. Are you trying to tell me I won't be able to cash a money order as late as ten or eleven in the morning because of a late-rising bank vault?"

The Western Union clerk shrugged and answered, "Hell, I'm not trying to tell you *nothing*. I just don't want you yelling at us if you can't get that much money in such an all-fired hurry. Do you want me to send these wires for you or not?"

Stringer told him to go ahead, paid at this end lest he piss off anyone at the other, and went back outside to amble back to his hotel. He paused in the doorway, bemused, as a corporal's squad of guardsmen marched a couple of shabby civilians past at bayonet point. He knew the feeling. He patted the breast pocket of his jacket to make sure he was still packing that military pass. Then he hauled the makings from the shirt pocket across the way and proceeded to build himself a smoke as he let his eyes adjust to the even less certain light. By now the sky above was as dark as it seemed likely to get, while the new-fangled and doubtless well-meant electrified street lighting even small towns went in for these days, took some getting used to.

Stringer and the rest of his generation had, it was true, grown up with the wonders of Thomas Alva Edison, but while the first electrical light bulb had winked on about the time Stringer was getting good with his first set of crayons and coloring books, it had taken him and the young electrical industry about the same amount of time to grow up. Stringer had been shaving regular before there'd been enough wiring strung to make the purchase of an Edison bulb worthwhile, save as a novelty to astound the neighbors with. But now that even small towns had their own generating plants, with all the arcane details of transformers, fuseboxes and such about worked out, nighttimes were sure getting hard on the nerves.

It wasn't as if he couldn't see anything or anybody clean across the way, as he sealed his smoke with his tongue and considered whether he wanted to light it or not, out here in the open like an infernal clay pigeon. He could see, hell, way down the block, provided anyone that far off didn't *mind* being seen. But thanks to the way the modern street lamps glared, each surrounded by its own halo of flying bugs, the *shadows* they cast were black as octopus ink and, while he wasn't worried about any octopus gunning for him, he did have to consider that one two-gun cuss he'd last met just about here.

Late night walks had been a heap simpler, if not safer, up until mighty recently. Whilst the streets of towns this size had been step-in-shit-dark after sundown, things had evened out more fair and square. If you couldn't see a cuss throwing down on you from more than ten yards off by lantern light, he couldn't see *you* any better. Stringer thoughtfully struck a match, lit his smoke, and stepped into an inky strip of shadow cast by a parked bakery wagon as he realized it worked both ways.

But he still liked the old ways better, when and if he suspected someone might be sore at him about something. He considered crawfishing away from the well-lit business street and making his way back to the Palace via a less illuminated route. Then he decided to do nothing at all for now, as he heard a distant gun go off and a mighty officious voice call out, "Freeze or you're dead, you fool Red!"

He nodded to himself and muttered, "Roundup Time in Cripple Creek. They didn't mention any curfew hours on those martial law posters, but we'd still best get our civilian ass off the street before we wind up arguing with that asshole colonel again!"

Suiting actions to his mutterings, Stringer cut across the street, to hell with who might be laying for him on the far side, and picked up his pace a bit as he strode toward his hotel. He flinched and cussed like a mule skinner when he suddenly found himself walking in step with that same infernal little Welsh gal again. He hadn't the least notion where she'd been lurking like one of the Little People before she'd popped out of nowhere in her misty mysterious way. So he was mostly cussing himself as a blind fool and she seemed to take the bad words in good grace, saying, "I took your message to our friends, look you. They can't meet you at your hotel or, indeed, anywhere this close to the center of things and those dreadful Colorado troops. For we've been betrayed again, you see, and they're arresting men, and women, too, just for standing up for their just desserts at the hands of those dreadful men who own the world all of us were born into."

Stringer didn't slow down, but tried to keep his tone friendly as he told her, "I don't want to get picked up by the military, either. You'd better slip back under your mushroom if you don't want to wind up in the stockade, sis. You just missed seeing them grab a couple of your boys and . . ."

"I did see and they weren't union men." She cut in, adding with a disdainful sniff, "Those hirelings of the mine owners wouldn't know Karl Marx from J.P. Morgan if they woke up in bed with either. They only have orders to grab anyone who's not wearing a starched shirt and silk necktie, you see. As if working for a living was a crime, look you!"

He grimaced and said, "I'm not sure I share your sentiments about the ownership of property, but I follow your drift and, since I'm not really dressed for the opera, I mean to run the rest of the way if it's all the same with you."

She grabbed his elbow, warning, "Don't you dare! There are riflemen staked out all about, just to see who might be running from their street patrols. You're never going to make it all the way back to the Palace without being stopped, look you. You'd better come with me. The darker streets the W.M.F. controls are ever so much safer, you see!"

He asked her, dryly, "Safer for who? No offense, sis, but I've already had one rain slicker shot up down in Colorado Springs and you should have seen the two-gun bozo I met up *here*, earlier this very evening." Then he reflected some on that and added, with a sigh, "Come to think of it, you likely have. Jack London warned me your union's sort of radical and he used to write Marxist pamphlets, before he found out what villains who published for profit were willing to pay."

She sounded disgusted as she told him, "You don't have to tell a union lass about the way the rich can tempt once-honest workers of this wicked world from the socialist path to salvation. I could tell you tales of men turning fink after years in the pits as well as the movement. But I'm only a messenger, you see. If you want to hear our side, you must come with me up the mountainside a bit, look you."

He was about to tell her what he thought of that suggestion when one of those new-fangled electrical search lights flashed on in both their faces and a superior-sounding but rather sissy voice called out, "Well, well, what have we here?"

Another voice on the far side of the blinding dazzle answered, in a more reasonable, tone, "I've seen both this cowhand and the, ah, lady he's with afore, Lieutenant. Neither one describes at all like that list of Reds we got from the Pinks, if you ask me."

The sneery voice replied, "Nobody's asking you, *Sergeant*. I'll be the judge of what's going on, here." Then he asked Stringer, "What's going on, here, cowboy?"

Stringer couldn't have sounded as sneery if he tried, but he didn't worry about sounding respectful as he answered, "I'm no more a cowhand than you are a soldier, if the truth would be known. I ride for the *San Francisco Sun* and you may as well know I can write mighty sarcastically about officious weekend warriors acting dumb. So don't act dumb with me and I won't act dumb with you. You want to see my press credentials and permit to be up here, covering all your daring deeds?"

"You'd *better* have something to show us, Mister," growled the shavetail in an even icier tone, adding, "You'd better have something *good* to show us, unless you and your, ah, lady friend enjoy bread and water, and not all that much of either, 'til the provost martial decides just how daring we're to treat such important folk."

So Stringer got out both his personal credentials and the pass issued in the name of the Colorado National Guard, no matter who'd signed the fool thing. He handed it to the sergeant, who passed it on to the shavetail. As the puffed-up young squirt shifted the beam to read the papers in his hand, Stringer could see them all a heap better. He reminded himself never to draw on anyone shining a search light in his face. For there must have been *ten* of the rascals all told. Then he had the papers back and the beam in his face again as the shavetail said, grudgingly, "All right, you don't seem to be a union tough after all. So what were you and this, ah, lady, doing so far from any respectable address at this hour?"

Stringer said, "We had to send a wire home for money. Prices up this way sure are outrageous. You can ask at Western Union if you want."

The beam swung from Stringer to sweep up and down the pretty but slightly shabby and disheveled young brunette. The officer murmured something to his sergeant, who not only murmured back but snickered, nastily. The shavetail flicked off his light, to save his batteries, most likely, since he wasn't any more polite as he told Stringer, "She frankly doesn't look that expensive, to me. But let's not argue about it. The two of you have let's say five minutes to get off my street. Are we likely to have any argument about that, ah, MacKail?"

Stringer answered, "Not hardly. Our hotel can't be three full minutes from here and we already noticed the Nickelodean's closed for the night. But do you mind telling us what time in the cold gray dawn this curfew's supposed to lift, Lieutenant?"

The part-time officer answered, "I'd stay off the street well after sunrise, if I was a stranger in town and had anything half as pretty to keep me company. The sergeant, here, will see the two of you back to your hotel. Don't let me see either of you until I'm off duty, hear?"

Stringer didn't argue and, since rank had its privileges no matter what the rank, the sergeant naturally detailed two troopers to escort Stringer and the girl they'd accepted as his girl back to the Palace. Neither had their Krags aimed impolite and any enlisted man had to be more sensible than a reservist who couldn't even make First John. So Stringer asked casually how come the Guard was cracking down so hard when, as far as he could see, nothing much seemed to be happening.

One out of two men always seemed talkative. So the trooper who was, in this case, told them, "The time to crack down on anarchist bomb throwers is before they throw any infernal bombs, not after. The Pinks have agents working undercover as usual and they just sent word that some famous anarchist bomber is fixing to blow something or someone up here in Cripple Creek."

The other trooper, as if not to be left out, chimed in with, "Them red radicals with the Big Bad Bill are mighty mean, even for malcontented hard rock men. So far they've kilt more than one spy the Pinks sent in to fink on 'em. But they can't kill everyone who comes to a secret meeting if they mean to hold any secret meetings at all. So we got a pretty good lead on 'em and should Big Bad Bill show his ugly mutt at this altitude, we'll have him right off!"

The girl had obviously been trying, but she suddenly just had to blurt, "What charge do you mean to arrest Big Bill Heywood on, look you? Can even the federal government arrest an American citizen just for belonging to a labor union or even the socialist party?"

Stringer wanted to kick her. But he could only crunch the small hand she'd hooked over his elbow as one of the tropper answered her, calmly enough, "You've been listening to union agitators on soap boxes, I see. I know the feeling. I used to think the red flaggers only wanted a fair deal for the working man until I read about the hard-working coppers they blowed up in that Haymarket Riot back in Chicago-Town. They said then they was demonstrating for an eight hour day. But dang their hides, they *got* their eight hour day off the mine owners the *last* time they caused such a commotion. So what might Big Bad Bill and his radicals want this time, if it ain't just trouble for the sake of trouble?"

She might have answered, if Stringer hadn't been twisting her thumb so hard. Between the pain and such common sense as she might have had, she managed to hold her tongue until they made it to the corner just this side of the hotel entrance and Stringer told the troopers, "We sure thank you for getting us home safe and sound through all those mad bombers, boys."

But it didn't work. One of the troopers insisted, "The sarge told us to see you to your door, folks."

Stringer smiled sheepishly and said, "Bueno. We'll just use the fire door around to the side then, if it's all the same with you and your sarge."

The older of the two part-time guardsmen chuckled. So Stringer took the lead as, behind them, the less wordly one whispered to his comrade, who whispered back, just loud enough to redden Stringer's ears, if not the mysterious girl's, "Use your imagination, country boy. This is as fancy a hotel as they have up this way, and you must have heard what the sarge told the louie *she* was."

The greener guardsman said, "Oh!" and snickered. The girl caught her breath but managed not to whirl on either of them. Meanwhile Stringer had tried the metal-sheathed side door and heaved a silent sigh of relief when it didn't turn out to be locked on the inside after all. Those new one-way panic bars a few of the better establishments in bigger towns had started to use were said to cost a bundle.

He got the Welsh girl inside and shut the fire door as politely in their faces as he felt they deserved. It was pretty dark indoors after that. But they seemed to be in the bottom of a stairwell and as he got his bearings Stringer told her, "I'm on the second floor, praise the Lord, for I doubt I'd be able to pass you off as my mother or maiden aunt in either the lobby or the billiard room. Let's go on up." To which she replied with an outraged gasp, "Up where? To a hotel room with yourself and no chaperone? And what kind of a lass do you think I am, good sir?''

He answered, simply, ''I don't know, yet. Would you rather take your chances with me or those troopers patroling outside, sis?''

She sniffed and said, ''I'm not your sister. I'd be Glynnis Rice, or Miss Rice, to you, if you don't mind. As for taking chances with any man at all . . . Well, then, if it's prison or perdition I suppose I'll have to choose perdition. For it's both I've suffered for the cause in my time and, all things being equal, being raped while in prison does take more out of a lass than just getting it over with and getting on with the true struggle, you see.''

He started to tell her the last thing he had in mind right now was a play for her fair white body, but as he led her up the dark stairs he reflected on the fact, as she no-doubt must have, that unless he meant to throw her to the wolves, he was stuck with her at least until they lifted that infernal curfew, hopefully around the time the mine whistles announced the morning shift, and meanwhile both of them were stuck with the simple fact that the bed upstairs was just about wide enough for two mighty good friends.

He knew a true gent would offer to sleep on the sofa, if only there was a sofa, or the floor because there wasn't, but she'd as much as accused him of being no such thing and, hell, it did seem a shame to be stuck with the name without the game. So he decided to leave it at Lady's Choice and see what happened.

What happened, once he had her up in his room with the door locked and the shades drawn, involved her flopping face down across the bed and blubbering, ''Oh, no, I can't go through with it, even for the cause, you see!'' To which he could only reply, with a weary sigh, ''I see you've claimed the only soft place to lie down, or even sit, you communistic little pest.''

CHAPTER NINE

Stringer would never know for certain how things might have gone with Glynnis if they hadn't both been startled out of their wits in the middle of an otherwise tedious conversation by the not too discreet rapping of knuckles and the downright rude rattle of the damn fool trying to get in at them at this hour, for whatever reason.

As the girl he'd smuggled up to his room stared pale and owl-eyed at him Stringer whispered, "Under the covers and let me do all the talking!" as he reached for the light switch near the locked door and called out, "Hold your damned horses out there. Let me get my damned breath and pants!" Then he switched off the overhead Edison bulb and proceeded to get rid of his hat, jacket and shirt as he added, "Who is it and what might you want, you unromantic cuss?"

A softer voice answered, "Keep it down, MacKail. This is a business call. A *private* business call if only we can keep it that way."

Stringer was pretty sure he recognized the voice. He still left his gun rig in place around his hips, plausible or not, as he cracked the door open wide enough to see it was Dutch Ritter out there all by himself. So he cussed but didn't really put up a real fight as the pushy mogul hissed, "Let me in! Things could get fucked up entirely if anyone told your backers about this little get-together, see?"

Stringer growled warningly, "Watch your lingo. Ladies present." Which inspired Ritter to let fly a nervous chuckle, tick his hat brim at the dark form in Stringer's bed, and smirk, "I admire a man who stays in training for sporting events. Murdstone got me to agree to an afternoon race because he said you needed time to gather nuts for that modest side bet. It was only later, after he'd been at the forty-rod a spell, he got around to telling us all you were a professional driver as well as a great author and lover."

Stringer growled, "You don't have to get personal to get out of covering my personal annoyance about your manners. But for the record be it known to one and all I didn't back off when I found out you were the swell sport with the professional fixing to race me up that mountain. I only had the brains to adjust Murdstone's gas and air feed to the altitude it was choking at. I reckon T.S. thought that made me some sort of mechanic. Do you still want out?"

Ritter laughed slyly and replied, "I never said I wanted out. I'd like to sort of deal you *in,* if only you'd stop leaping to conclusions and give a body the chance to spread some cards on the table."

Stringer said, "I figured it was either that or the other. If you don't want to call off the honest wager, don't even hint at anything dishonest, Dutch. Aside from being a reporter, I've never liked tinhorns who cheat, even when I didn't have a paper to expose them in."

Ritter gasped as if he'd been stung by a bee and demanded, "Now who ever said anything about cheating?" To which Stringer replied with a dry but not unkind chuckle, "I just stopped you before you could tell me how much you liked me, how sorry you felt that after all my labors I only had a thousand to bet and how easy it would be for me to bet with you instead of against you, on the side, at, ah, much better odds?"

Ritter laughed, too innocently by half, and said, "Hell, old son, I know better than to try and fix a race with an infernal newspaper reporter. But, say someone was to make you such an offer, I don't suppose you'd like to guess at what your price might be, every man having his price, as surely a newspaperman should know?"

Stringer nodded soberly and said, "My price is a million dollars. It's been that ever since I got caught swiping candy as a kid. After my dad finished our discussion in the woodshed he sat me down, gave me his kerchief to wipe my fool face, and told me never to sin no more for less than a million dollars. So I never have. It was fixed in my mind early that you feel mighty small getting caught for one fool penny less than real money."

Ritter didn't laugh. He said, "You get your first million stealing those pennies, one at a time. You're going to lose that thousand, too, Don Quixote. Take it from a man with fewer ideals and a heap more common sense!"

Then he let himself out before Stringer could throw him out, so Stringer locked the door after him and, leaving the light out, moved over to the window and raised the shade, telling the girl in his bed, "That was too long a story to go into. Let's just see if the coast is clear, now, and we'll see about getting you back under your mushroom."

Then he swore again and muttered, "This just doesn't seem to be my night!" Two National Guardsmen were jawing under a lamppost, right across the street. He told her so, adding, "If we can't make a run for it soon we'd best not even try. I doubt even that military pass would get me through alone after midnight. Those part-time soldiers are really on the prod. Pinkerton's tip-off seems to have them more worried than the mine owners. I just met some M.O.A. leaders downstairs and they're all fixing to watch a motor car race instead of their fool mines.''

She said, ''That's what my friends wanted to talk to you about. As there's no way for me to take you to them, now, I'll just have to do my best as spokeswoman for the working classes of the world, so pull that shade back down and get in bed with me, look you.''

He followed her advice, figuring, even as he sat on the edge of the mattress to shuck his boots and gunbelt that she'd meant that more platonic than it had sounded. He'd already noticed she'd hauled off her high-buttons and that wispy summer dress, but he naturally figured she still had her shimmy and underdrawers on, as he hung his gun over a bed post where it would be handy, and explained, ''I got to get these boots off because the spurs might play hell with the bedding.''

But as he rolled under the quilts with her in just his jeans he discovered right off, the bed being that narrow, she hadn't been wearing any shimmy or underdrawers under that raggedy one-piece dress. It sure felt awkward, wearing pants, with a stark naked little gal built so big where it mattered snuggled up against one's bare chest, murmuring, ''You'll take it easy, at first, won't you? I fear it's been a while, and to tell the truth, I was only married a short while before my dear one was shot by the company men so long ago and far away.''

Not knowing how to answer in words, he kissed her, and whether he was supposed to take it easy or not, she didn't seem to give a damn about even the copper rivets trying to hold his jeans together as she ripped them off with her hot little hands and pressed her hot little body against the results, sobbing, even as he wondered whether he was entering her of his own free will or being swallowed alive, "Oh, do be gentle with me, good sir!"

Which made him slow down a mite, until she dug her nails into his bare bounding buttocks and moaned, "Don't *tease* me so! If you must have your way with me can't you try to pleasure me at the same time, you cruel exploiter of the weaker half of humankind?"

He didn't answer. It wouldn't have been too romantic if he'd let her know how inspired he was by such bullshit as he spread her slim but surprisingly muscular thighs as wide as they'd go, hooked over his elbows, and felt a lot more inspired by her firm young body than the mushy thinking she'd obviously been exposed to by way of any education at all. Once he'd brought her to full climax that way, and some other ways she seemed as delighted by, she began to respond in kind without uncalled-for remarks about who might be exploiting whom, with what, in what, and by the time they had to pause for a smoke and the repose that went with it, she confided it had felt just lovely and that she wouldn't mind being exploited again, if he really wanted more. Stringer got the Bull Durham he'd rolled for them lit up and going good enough, considering he'd rolled it one handed in the dark, before he told her, "We'd better discuss less enjoyable labor conflict, first. You said you had something to tell me about the big strike up this way. So far, no offense, your union and the National Guard seem more excited about it than either the mine owners or the crews they still have working their mines for 'em and, in any case, why me and not, say, someone like Bert Carlton?"

She asked him who Bert Carlton was. He blew smoke out his nose like a fly-bit bull and growled, "Jesus H. Christ, you're out to shut down the Cripple Creek gold fields and you don't know the name of the big shot fighting to keep 'em open? Carlton is the head of the M.O.A. and likely has as much to say about running the state troops as the state governor. I wish I could get someone to bet me Bert Carlton doesn't know who Big Bill Heywood is, and I don't run *anything*! So why does your union keep blowing holes in my rain slicker? What in thunder am I supposed to know that Bert Carlton and even that second lieutenant with the flashlight, bless him, doesn't already know?"

She giggled and groped for his flaccid privates as she told him, "I'm glad he got us into these unexpected surroundings, too. But I fear I'm as in the dark as you about anyone blowing holes in your dear raincoat. What the lads want from you is a fair hearing, or should I say a printing. Some of them who served in Cuba say you wrote the truth about the dreadful sanitary conditions and the writing of great deeds that never happened, even though you might have wound up ever so much richer than some famous newspapermen who covered the war from Sloppy Joe's in Havana."

He put the rolled smoke to her lips as he mused, half to himself, "Well, maybe it was a splendid little war, as Dick Davis put it, for the boys who sipped all that Bacardi well behind the lines. But the War with Spain and even the last showdown up here in Cripple Creek are stale news, you naughty-fisted little thing." Then he took back the butt and repeated, "What *have* I missed, if anything?" So she told him, "Our side of the argument. We've spent over ten thousand in hard-earned union dues, trying to get the story out before the public, but so far only the socialist papers nobody else ever reads have printed a word in our favor."

He smiled thinly and said, "Why should anyone? Marx said it all in his Manifesto of 1848 and missed a few important points about human nature way back then. My pal and rival, Jack London, came near to dying of starvation trying to improve on Marx before he found out folk would rather read about sled dogs. You're right about the circulation figures of the left-wing rags, even printed in English. Those English Reds, H.G. Wells and G.B. Shaw, have done a lot better since they wised up and started writing for the general public. Shaw was living off his wife, Fabian Socialist or not, 'til he made a name for himself covering the Jack The Ripper Case for the London Times and as for old Wells . . ."

"Never mind those turncoats!" She cut in, giving his poor dong an almost painful jerk as she continued, "We want you to publish the truth in a mainstream publication the general public reads. It's not fair of the mine owners to paint us as black-bearded red anarchists when all we demand is decent working conditions at decent pay!"

He reached his free hand down to help her inspire him to friendlier feelings, toward *her*, at least, as he just had to observe, "Unless I've missed something, not too many people who pay union dues instead of collecting 'em are apt to feel your hard rock lads are abused enough to justify Harry Orchard's brand of labor negotiations, doll. You got the eight-hour shift at three bucks a shift the *last* time you busted things up. Most working stiffs in this land of opportunity are still putting in twelve hour days at around a buck a day. Your miners make twice the day wages of a skilled carpenter and thrice the monthly pay of a fair cowhand. Do you really expect a trolley car driver drawing twelve bucks a week to weep bitter tears over a poor exploited miner pulling down eighteen?"

She let go his treasure to protest in a union hall tone, "It's not the same! Grubbing for gold in the bowels of the earth is deadly dangerous and beyond human endurance as well!"

He shrugged his bare shoulders, bobbing her disheveled head gently as he did so, saying, "If it was unendurable, nobody would do it. I grew up in gold mining country, kiddo. So I likely know as much or more as any girl, no offense, about the heat and stale air down yonder. Why did you think I was willing to work cows for less money to begin with? Most folk don't know what it's like in mine or, hell, down a well. Most don't care to find out. That's why the M.O.A. offers higher than usual day wages to lure common laborers up into these mountains. I don't see many quitting, and the mine owners seems to be able to replace those who do, even offering less than the wages they agreed to, last strike.''

She tried, ''That was before the turn of the century, look you! The cost of living has risen, since.'' But he just told her, ''Not really. Things cost more when I was a kid. Mass production and the big business depression of those not-so-gay-nineties drove prices *and* wages down to where they've barely began to recover and, meanwhile, every steamer coming in across the pond brings more greenhorns willing to bust rock or, hell, chop cotton, for less than the second generation American *can* get by on. I shouldn't have to tell a lady who talks so Taffy just how many hard rock miners are already out here, fresh from the old countries. I'll file any story as it takes place, Glynnis, and I'll call things as I see 'em. But as long as you're running messages back and forth, you may as well tell your side that this time dynamiting could be a real mistake. You don't have that much public sympathy, even from the mining folk, this time around. The owners and the state government they own are just dying for the chance to take off the gloves and bust your union with bare knuckles, butt stock and bayonet. If I were Big Bill Heywood I'd send old Harry Orchard and his toughs back under the wet rocks they crawled out from under!''

She sighed and said, ''If only we *could*, look you! That's part of our side we'd like you to put in the papers for us, dear heart. Lads of the rank and file never voted for the likes of that dreadful Harry Orchard, or even Big Bill with his dreadful bragging about blood and slaughter. Dear Charley Moyer, more a working man than a Marixst, is the one true head of the W.F.M. You have to get that message out for us. It's the radical wing of the movement, the ones more interested in destroying Capitalism than improving the lot of the common man, who make all the soap box speeches that cause so much trouble for our cause. Charley Moyer doesn't want to shut down the gold fields. He just wants the M.O.A. to agree to an all-union work force up here in the Rockies. Can you deny that some mine owners, if not all, pay less than the going rate agreed to back in '93?''

He told her, gently, ''I don't have to agree to anything. I've never owned a *coal* mine. Your Charley Moyer's not going to own his union, either, if he doesn't get his own soap box, soon. For, no matter where Big Bill Heywood really stands on your union ladder, he's making all the noise and, as far as I can see, calling all the shots. I did spy Harry Orchard slithering into one of your union meetings the other night, whether Moyer knows he's out this way or not. Whether the law can prove it or not, we all know Orchard's killed more poor souls than Wild Bill and Billy The Kid combined, although, come to study on it, back-shooting women and children might not count on such scorecards.''

She insisted, ''That dreadful Orchard brute is not on the payroll of the W.F.M., look you!'' as she took fond hold of him again, as if to reassure him of her good faith. He didn't want to argue about the sins of an ugly union thug half as much as he wanted to kiss one of their female members some more, so he snubbed out the Bull Durham, took her in his arms again, and just said, ''He's on *some* damned body's payroll and leave us not forget my poor old yellow slicker got shot full of holes the night he blew into town. But as long as you say he's not with your bunch, I won't hold any hard feelings against you.'' Which made her laugh like hell for some reason, and then he had to laugh, too, as he followed her drift. For whilst he wasn't exactly holding it against her, it felt hard enough inside her for both of them to forget about other unrest for quite a spell.

CHAPTER TEN

Cocks crowed, wagons rolled, and the next morning Glynnis was up and out of there before the sun got high enough to matter. Stringer was already beginning to miss her by the time he'd showered, shaved and stuffed his gut downstairs. He missed her more when he got over to the Western Union office. The pretty blonde was on duty again and her eyes were sort of red-rimmed, too, which inspired him to wonder how much sleep she'd had herself, doing what with that other lucky cuss between times. But he was too polite to ask about her own personal problems and his just seemed to be beginning as she handed over two Western Union money orders, but not one dime of cash he could wager or waste some other way. She repeated what the night man had said about the infernal bank, but since it was just across the way and the money orders were made out in his name to begin with, Stringer offered to do his own fetching and carrying.

That turned out to be more of a chore than he'd bargained for. First, he had to convince the prune-faced, four-eyed branch manager he was exactly who he said he was, which was only easy whilst dealing with sensible human beings, and then the cruel-smiling old fart shot a Chessie-cat grin at the big clock on the wall above the bank of teller's cages to say, "We can't get into the vault for that kind of cash before that clock over there reads nine A.M."

That only sounded reasonable until Stringer recalled what the old fashioned Regulator clock at Western Union had read, hauled out his own pocket watch to confirm it, and said, "Hold on. According to my Ingersol here and Western Union yonder, it's already going on quarter to ten and my pony and me have us a train to catch this morning!"

The banker nodded agreeably enough but explained, "That's an electric clock. The power was off a while in the wee small hours, I fear. For as you can see, the dial only reads eight thirty-five."

Stringer nodded and said, "I just as much as said your fool clock is running slow, fancy as it may look. What's wrong with the clocks we've always had? The Seth Thomas my Granddaddy brought west back in '49 still ticks off the right time, day and night, on the mantle of my Uncle Don back to Calaveras County."

The banker pursed his lips and said something about having to keep up to date, even though he looked too old to have known Queen Victoria in the Biblical sense. Stringer grimaced and said, "I must be missing something, here. What has a slow electricated clock to do with this damn bank sitting on my money this damned late in the damned old day?"

The banker said, "Nothing, directly. But the time lock on our vault downstairs is regulated by an electric clock as well. Naturally, it's running just as slow this morning, due to the same power failure late last night. You'll just have to be patient with us for a few more minutes, Mister MacKail."

Stringer grunted, "I can see I have to, but I sure

wish modern science would either slow down or get as wonderful as the tabloids keep saying it is.'' Then he brightened and asked, ''Say, wouldn't a vault kept locked by electric power just sort of spring open, all by itself, if someone was to shut said power off?''

The banker shot him a superior smile and answered, ''Give us credit for some common sense, sir. What possible use could even a tobacco shop have for a lock any kid could open just by cutting a wire or, pulling a plug? Our time lock's electrical timer is connected to a circle of bolts that are moved quite simply by electromagnets. The idea is to make it simply impossible to open the vault, even with the proper combination, during the hours our armed guards are not on duty. When the timer has been *set* to let us or anyone else into the vault, the magnets switch on to draw the bolts. They're not *on* when the vault's supposed to be locked, so naturally . . .''

''I follow your drift,'' sighed Stringer, unable to resist adding, ''It still sounds more complicated than it needs to be. I'd already have my damned money if you boys weren't so all-fired modern, no offense.''

The banker glanced up at the slow clock again, saying, ''None taken. The Wild Bunch may or may not be hitting banks and stopping trains all over the Rockies this summer, but suffice it to say they won't get into *our* vault, even if they shoot us all down like dogs. Did you hear how dumb Butch Cassidy looked that time he tried to blow the up-to-date strongbox on the U.P. Flier a year or so back?''

Stringer grinned despite himself and said, ''Yep, and when you're right you're right. You have to admit he finally got it open, with all that extra dynamite, but I'll allow shredded money floated down out of the sky for hours afterwards. So I'd best just go have me a beer whilst my own money and modern science catches up with us.''

He actually had two at the saloon across the way,

keeping one eye on yet another old-fashioned clock, this one even possessing a swell cuckoo, that told the damned time close enough without any infernal electric bills to worry about.

Then, still having a few minutes to spare and not wanting to waste any more of his life talking to that musty old banker, he strolled over to the livery, had them saddle and bridle his bay cow pony, and rode it back to the bank around ten thirty, real time, or quarter past nine the way electrical clocks seemed to run in these parts. He tethered the pony out front, went in, and this time they gave him his money, grudgingly, after making him sign what amounted to an application for a damned job with their damned bank.

Stringer knew better than to carry that much dinero where anyone else could get at it without risking mutual destruction. So he had his side bet in the lining of his right boot as he mounted up out front and rode for the railroad yards, where Murdstone was supposed to meet up with him this side of eleven, so he might have shown up a mite late in any case. Then a female scream made him turn in the saddle just in time to see a pony cart full of little kids tear past him lickety split, drawn by what he took for a large mad dog until, on second glance, he saw it looked more like a shaggy chestnut pony, frothing even worse at the mouth as it ignored the attempts of the young gal at the reins to control it. Stringer spurred his own mount in pursuit, shaking out a loop of grass rope without thinking as he considered the railroad yards and tailing tips the way the fool brute was running with the bit in its teeth and Lord only knew what in its jug head.

If it didn't stop or somebody didn't stop it this side of the mounds of wildly eroded mine waste, or tailings, on the far side of the yards, that overloaded cart was never going to make it through on its own two wheels. But what the hell, the *tracks* would likely turn the fool cart over after shaking the poor little rascals dishrag-limp, first. So Stringer commenced swinging a community loop above his Stetson as he lit out after the runaway, knowing that he'd have no more than one throw before the problem became grimly academic. A little girl in the back saw him coming after them and called out, "Oh, help us, mister!" which inspired the grown redhead at the reins to shoot him a terrified glance over one calico-clad shoulder. He called out, "Don't look at *me*! Watch where you're *going* and, while you're at it, *duck!*"

She did, and he threw; it seemed to take a million years, and he was sure he'd blown it as his big loop floated out ahead of him like a lazy giant smoke ring over the bouncing cart, and then his loop settled prize money perfect around the front end of that shaggy brown son of a bitch and Stringer reined in hard, hoping to bust the brute good as his own pony, bless its mispent youth, dug all four hooves into the dusty gravel, braced for the shock.

It was a good one, rougher on the runaway than Stringer and his semiretired cow pony, for while the grass rope twanged taut with a report that would have busted any reata ever braided by Anglo or Mex, Stringer's bay kept its balance while the runaway had the pony cart slammed into its shaggy rump harder than hell. So, like most brats, it responded to a good slap on the ass by bawling, in horse, and just standing there docile as a stuffed toy while Stringer swung out of the saddle and hand over hand up the rope to administer a good punch on the muzzle and a savage yank on the runaway's bridle while the brute went on bawling and the gal up in the cart called out, "Don't punish him, sir! He didn't know what he was doing!"

Stringer unbuckled the bridle's cheek strap on his side to run the bit up past the brute's rear molars, where it damned well belonged, as he called back, "I'm not punishing anybody, ma'am, albeit the fool who last fastened this bridle sure deserves a good boot in the never-mind."

She blushed pretty as a rose as she asked what was wrong with the way their pony had been bridled. He suspected he knew who'd done the dumb deed, but he contented himself with, "You can get away with a loose bit in the mouth of a halfway *sane* critter, ma'am. But let a mean one with neither mercy nor brains take the bit in its teeth and, well, you just found out what can happen. So let's say no more about it for now."

She still told him she and the children were ever so grateful as he tightened the far strap, socked the brute in the muzzle another time to remind it this was a man's world, damn it, and removed his thrown rope, saying, "Let's not get all mushy about it. You ought not to have any more trouble with this homicidal maniac. So forgive me if I get my own fool self on down the road, ma'am. I'd be more than proud to see you all safe to your destination, under ordinary circumstances, but right now I'm destined to catch me a train."

Then he headed back to his own patient mount, coiling the rope up again as he strode. Behind him the gal with all the kids said something about trains. He just kept going and, when he got there, he was glad he had. For he found T.S. Murdstone doing a sort of war dance on the freight platform and when Stringer dismounted and joined him there, more calmly, Murdstone said, "You just made it. The Panard's already in yon boxcar and how come you brung along that damned horse?"

Stringer said, "I had to. You weren't figuring on giving me that motor car to get back in if I win that race with it, were you?"

CHAPTER ELEVEN

If Stringer had passed the place before, he hadn't missed much by paying more attention to the gold camp road he was following for the first time. The junction where one changed to the cog railroad up to the summit of Pikes Peak was little more than a cluster of small frame business opportunities clustered around the dinky railroad depot.

Stringer concentrated on the comfort of his livery bay and the safety of his few belongings in its saddle bags while the others saw to getting their own gear, including the two motor cars, off the CS&CCRR. The sweet-talking but mean-looking old lady who sold post cards, Coca Cola and stuffed horned toads across from the loading platform of the cog train told him he could leave the bay in her barn out back for two bits a day. By the time he'd attended that chore and rejoined the others nearer the tracks, the combination bound for Colorado Springs was chugging off for the big city, and T.S. Murdstone was kicking the red tires of his Panard and cussing fit to bust while most of the others, the others being around two dozen members of the local sporting fraternity, were either offering T.S. condolances or laughing outright. Stringer didn't laugh as he joined them, even though a horseless carriage with four flat tires did look sort of comical, unless you had *money* riding on the dumb-looking machine. Stringer did. Everyone with money to wager had handed it to the respected, armed and dangerous Bert Carlton for safe keeping and redistribution, pending the outcome of the race. Carlton wasn't betting, himself. He'd said the Panard and Buick fixing to race each other up the skinny dirt road to Summit Lodge looked evenly matched to him, and that he didn't see much future in the horseless carriage to begin with. That had been before the Panard's tires had all gone mysteriously flat while both machines had been carried this far in unguarded box cars. Through a gap in the crowd, Stringer spied Dutch Ritter, part of his big blue Buick, and all of the little squirt he'd hired to beat Murdstone's Panard up the mountain, whether it could climb mountains on flat tires or not. Neither Ritter nor the rat-faced little shit who'd likely let all the air out of those tires seemed to notice Stringer staring at them so severely. Ritter was waving a pocket watch about and mouthing off about icy conditions near the top of the mountain after dark. But the firmer-jawed and apparently fairer-minded head of the M.O.A. announced for all to hear, "There will be no race until and unless we can hold one fair and square."

There was a mutter of general agreement from the sporting gents assembled. Carlton held up a hand for silence and said, "For openers, we'll want witnesses to a fair start as well as a fair ending to this here automotive contest. So I suggest half or more of us take the cog train to the top, with neither of these horseless carriages to start up before the boys getting there the easy way have a right smart start on 'em."

Nobody argued with that. It sounded fair enough. But Murdstone bitched, "Hold on, now, Bert. Me and

MacKail, here, may need some time to get these infernal wheels stuffed with air again! I can't even say, 'til I rustle up a pump and test the inner tubes in a water trough whether we're dealing with punctures or whether some son of a bitch who shall be nameless, if only to keep this contest more mechanical than fatal, let the air out on purpose."

Ritter bulled closer to smile jeeringly at Murdstone and say, "You're right, you sore loser, for nobody calls this child a cheat unless he aims to prove it or fill his fist!"

The more reasonable Bert Carlton, who had less to lose either way, got between them to sooth, "Nobody's accusing nobody of nothing, *yet*. Why don't you try pumping your tires back up. T.S.?" To which Murdstone replied in a small sheepish voice, "I don't have a pump."

Even the judicious Carlton had to chuckle. Stringer caught himself grinning and then cussed Murdstone's family tree all the way back to that ape who hadn't passed on a lick of common sense to his fat descendents. Ritter couldn't resist rubbing it in by saying, "I have a pump along with a full tool kit in the trunk of my no-bullshit motor car, for whoever heard of driving one without even a tire pump to call one's own? It's small wonder you ain't up to driving up the mountain *yourself*, T.S."

Stringer had to agree with his otherwise mighty stupid betting partner when Murdstone wailed, "That's as dumb as it is unfair, coming from a man who hires girl-sized jockies to race his pile of junk!"

Bert Carlton sushed one and all to say, "We come to watch a race, not to listen to a slanging match. How's about lending T.S. your tire pump long enough to get things started fair and square, Dutch?"

Ritter shook his head and said, "Not hardly. I paid for my own education, let anyone betting against me pay for their own. You just said you and the boys rode all this way to watch a race, Bert. So let the record show me and Dusty Rhodes, driving for our side, stand ready to start our engine and get on with it, any damn time you say!"

Somewhere a brass bell was clanging. It seemed too loud and tuneful for a cow and, sure enough, when Stringer craned to stare that way above the crowd he saw the peanut roaster engine of the cog railroad was easing its quartet of slanty cars into the depot to drop off passengers from the top and pick up any who wanted to get up there in time to watch the sunset from fourteen thousand feet in the same sunny sky. Bert Carlton hauled out his own watch and consulted it before he announced, "We're running out of time to argue. I can't see sending anyone all the way up to watch the end of a race I can't see starting, at the rate we're going. How do you all feel about just calling it no contest, all bets off?"

Dutch Ritter demanded, "What difference does it make whether a motor car breaks down during or before a race? Would you call it all bets off if my boy missed a turn halfway to the top, damn it?"

Carlton grimaced and said, "I'd call it an occasion to send flowers, having seen how steep some of them hairpin turns drop off. But it ain't the same, Dutch. A runner tripping on the way to the wire and a runner who can't even start to run are not the same call, to my way of thinking."

But Ritter said, "They are to mine. My motor car and driver are ready to go. If the other side ain't, they forfeits their bets. You can look it up."

The head of their association scowled and demanded, "*Where*, for God's sake?" But Stringer had been thinking while everyone else had been arguing. So he asked, quietly, "Do we have, let's say, half an hour before the race has to begin, Mister Carlton?" To be told with a puzzled smile, "Hell, take forty-five minutes if you've a mind to. Just don't let me send these other gents up the mountain by cog train unless you know you're fixing to start after 'em *some* damned time!"

Stringer nodded and said he'd be right back. Then he bulled through the crowd toward the general store he'd spotted across from the place he'd left his pony. Asking inside if they had any tire pumps had been worth a try, even if the old goat behind the counter did laugh mighty rudely. Stringer bought throw rope, a lot of throw rope, instead, and met Murdstone in the doorway as he was heading back with his somewhat unusual automotive supplies. Murdstone said, "The sons of bitches have all gone up the mountain by cog rail, all but Bert and a few others who wanted to watch the beginning. But you'll never guess what I just found under the seat of my fool Panard! I didn't even know it folded forwards like so. One of the others over yonder said he'd read where some horseless carriages had tool kits built-in like so and, anyway, we don't have to worry about fluffing up my tires no more."

Stringer started to agree. Then he hefted the coils of stiff springy manila twist he'd just bought and said, "We're talking tires that may or may not have been seriously damaged, on a rocky road at high altitude where Lord knows what the proper pressure ought to be. So with your permission I aim to make *sure* those tires don't go flat on us again."

Murdstone never got around to giving his direct permission and the rat-faced Dusty Rhodes assured his own patron that Stringer was crazy as they all watched what he was doing, some in the crowd even helping as each wheel was jacked in turn and each inner tube got replaced by coiled rope under the red rubber casing. The whole chore took a little under an hour and then they were off, or at least Dusty Rhodes was off in that flashy blue Buick as Stringer tried in vain to start the infernal Panard with Murdstone at the throttle and him cranking. The cranking seemed to result in back-fires louder than a twelve gauge could manage, even when the backlash of the crank didn't threaten to break Stringer's arm. He kept checking the way Murdstone had the spark and choke levers set, and though they seemed right, the results remained about the same while Ritter's rival machine became a tiny blue dot way the hell up the rising slope. Stringer finally got the softer Murdstone to trade places with him. He saw he'd made a mistake when T.S. cranked the engine like a damned sissy. Then a mine owner who'd worked with his hands before finding his fortune told T.S. to let *him* give it a whirl and the engine caught on his first try. So as everyone near the bottom of the slope shouted their blessings or their curses, depending on how they'd bet, Stringer threw the French machine in gear and lit out after Dusty Rhodes, who seemed to be living up to his nickname if that was his dust, Jesus, over a mile up the wagon trace already!

Then, as he steered around the first serious turn and felt the rope-stuffed rear wheels sliding sideways on the dusty gravel roadway, Stringer saw he'd have to pay more attention to the motor car he was driving if he meant to drive it anywhere near the top. For while he'd driven these contraptions before, albeit on much straighter roads, it was all too easy to forget how *brainless* a horseless carriage ran, next to the real thing. For even that runaway pony cart he'd stopped earlier, had been tear-assing to destruction behind a critter, loco or not, who'd no-doubt draw the line at smashing head first into a brick wall or running smack off the road into blue sky. Stringer's generation had in fact learned to drive mostly behind much more sensible horse power that tended to get you home safe, drunk, sober or screwing. Perched in this speeding Panard, with nothing out in front of him but more sharp turns, he knew this *new* breed of travel called for the traveller keeping a sharper eye on where he might be going than travelers had ever been called upon before. As he swung around a barn-sized boulder to find himself staring ahead at a hundred-mile view of the high plains to the east, he swore, swerving sharply to his left and as the Panard skidded sideways gunned the engine for more traction, hoping that pool hall advice might work and, when it did, just inches from the edge, he swore and added, ''Jesus, this is worse than that chariot race in Governor Wallace's book about Ben Hur and we haven't even gotten to the steep climbing yet!''

Staring up the rocky slopes ahead he couldn't, in fact, tell just where on the mountain he might be now. Pikes Peak rises in a series of undulations, great and small, so some rises and dips you don't even notice, viewing the whole massif from any distance, turn into good-sized hills in their own right, bouncing *over* them.

By the same token, while the wagon trace ran nowhere along the edge of a sheer drop to sea level, those more modest but steep enough inclines the roadway *did* flirt with offered plunges sure to bust anybody going over the edge to smithereens. A couple of times he glimpsed the remains of wagons, way down, that had gone off in the past to be smashed and scattered among the boulders and juniper scrub. For they were above Timberline now, and so far he hadn't caught so much as a blue flash of that other son of a bitch in that other son of a bitching motor car!

Unless he spied it somewhere down *below* him, Stringer knew there was no way now, to beat the nasty but knowledgeable professional up this nasty single lane road to the sky. But whether he lost or not, halfway up had to be the dumbest place to stop, so he just had to keep going. At least he did until the engine started to cough and sputter on the steeper rises. He stopped in a draw before it could really die on him and left the drive train in neutral while he got out and got cracking, telling the gasping tin beast, ''Just hold on, damnit. We have to be more than ten thousand feet up and to tell the truth *my* lungs are commencing to feel it, too.'' As he readjusted the carburetor yet again he added, ''If they're ever going to seriously race these things cross-country, they're going to have to race 'em with two-man crews, one to keep the engine going and one to keep 'em on the road. I wish I was better at both, for I feel dumb as hell about that money I bet on us, now, Mademoiselle Panard!"

He got the engine purring again, climbed back aboard, and lit out after Dusty Rhodes, if that was the little shit's name. Stringer couldn't decide whether he'd seen that shifty rat-face before, perhaps on a reward poster, or whether the motor jocky was just a type one saw around race tracks and pool halls for some reason old Charley Darwin might be able to explain. Such human rodents hardly seemed cut out to make it among more *wholesome* competition.

Stringer didn't like the way the fuel needle waved at him as the grade got ever steeper. He was sure he'd started this infernal climb on a full tank and, hell, the critter had to get at least twenty miles to the gallon unless he'd read all those promises in the papers wrong. One of the main selling points of the horseless carriage was how cheap it was to keep one, next to a horse and buggy, whether one drove every day or not, for out on the road or out back in its stall, a horse had to be fed and watered more than once a day, seven days a week. But some still argued that whilst filling up a gas tank and just forgetting about it for days at a time was sure less troublesome than keeping a live critter, the oil and gasoline cost way more than water and oats. Old John D. and those gushers gushing clean out to the west coast now, had cut the cost of rock oil products, but nobody could afford to burn gasoline at the rate *this* infernal machine seemed to be burning it. So once more Stringer stopped, with the motor running idle, to get down and see if perhaps the cap of the fuel tank had come unstuck or something.

It was something *dirty*, he saw, after he'd tried the cap, found it screwed on tight, and gotten fixed to just go on and do his best before he'd sniffed, blinked, and hunkered down to stare soberly at the cluster of dusty spit balls in the gravel betwixt the rope-stuffed rear wheels. Another drop of gasoline plopped down to gather its own cocoon of flour-fine and cobweb gray dust as Stringer swore and ran his hand under the tank to discover that, sure enough, there was a wee pinhole bleeding drop by drop, enough to matter somewhere betwixt here and the top, even if he managed to get there without the leaky tank catching fire on him!

He rummaged under the rear seat everyone but him and the owner of the damned Panard seemed to have heard about. He didn't need the spanking new or at least unused air pump. The rope trick had given him a rough but solid ride up to now. He was looking for some of that rubber tape they sold for fixing inner tubes, fuel lines and so forth. But there wasn't any. He wondered, idly, how come there was half a pack of spearmint gum, made by that Yankee outfit in Chicago, if nobody had been under the back seat since they'd built the fool machine in *France*. But stopping that damned leak was more important right now than the history of the leaky motor car, or even how it had gotten to leaking everything from tire pressure to its infernal fuel, so he popped a couple of sticks of chewing gum in his mouth and while he tried to soften the stale shit with some effort and spit, had a look-see at the dipstick, to discover he was a tad low on crankcase oil as well!

As long as he had to crawl under anyway, Stringer checked the drain plug of the crankcase, swore, and tightened it hard as he could with the pliers he'd been smart enough to crawl under with. Then he stuck the wad of gum to the bottom of the fuel tank, rubbing it in hard with his now mighty greasy fingers. He couldn't tell if it was fixing to hold or not. He could only wipe his hands in the road dust until they looked more filthy than slippery, and get back up to do what he might about the damned mountain, now that he had the Panard running more reasonably. He was sure he'd lost the race, by now, of course. Dusty Rhodes had not only started well ahead of him but hadn't had to keep stopping, unless he'd sabotaged his own machine as well. Stringer could only keep plugging away, braced for the ribbing he was in for once he got to the top, if ever he *got* to the damned top. It had to be somewhere up ahead. But each time he caught sight of a good-sized bulge against the cobalt blue sky above, he found out once he got there, that there was another one just like it rising even higher. So, as he slowly drove up yet another steep incline, at full throttle, he was braced to see more mountain, or with any luck the windswept shingles of Summit Lodge. He'd found out what it looked like at that postcard shop more than a mile below and a lot more miles sideways, so he was more than a little surprised to see Dutch Ritter's big blue Buick silently blocking the narrow right-of-way ahead, with the booted feet of its wiry little driver sticking out from under the running board.

By the time Stringer braked to a stop near the rear bumper, Dusty Rhodes was out from under and back on his feet, with a nickel-plated Harrington & Richardson .32 in one hand. Stringer called out, "Howdy. Air getting too thin up here for Miss Buick's delicate lungs, Dusty?"

The smaller but dangerous acting Rhodes snarled, "Never mind what's wrong with *my* engine. You just cut your *own*, if you know what's good for you, MacKail!"

Stringer had to study on that as he stared soberly at the unwinking gun muzzle trained on him from mighty dicey range. His own gun was closer, of course, and threw heavier lead. But while Stringer felt no false modesty about his own quick draw, there were limits to how fast one could get one's own gun out, let alone aimed and fired, and this sure looked like one of them.

So he said, "You got the drop on me, Dusty. But would you mind telling me what you hope to prove by behaving so unsociable?"

The rival driver snapped, "The summit's just a few hundred feet over that next damned rise. I've been up here before. But it may as well be another ten miles, with *both* our engines stopped. So stop your engine. I'll kill you if you don't cut that switch!"

He sounded like he meant it. So Stringer grimaced, switched off the ignition, and as they were both enveloped in snow-scented stillness, told the rat-faced Rhodes, wistfully, "I've heard of sore losers but you're a real shit, no offense. Wasn't it enough to let the air out of my tires and fix this poor bucket of bolts to leak both oil and gas?"

The runt holding him at gunpoint looked sincerely puzzled as he answered, not too nicely, "I don't know what you're talking about. It don't matter. With neither machine able to make to the top, all bets are off."

Then he moved closer, keeping his whore pistol trained on Stringer every step of the way as he added, "Get out, hands polite, if you aim to view the sunset from up yonder this evening."

Stringer said that sure sounded poetic and climbed down from the driver's seat as Rhodes moved in, covering him every step of the way, to reach for the Panard's starting crank and hurl it way the hell off and down Pikes Peak with a backhand throw Stringer hadn't known the little shit had in him. As the crank rang tauntingly in ever-softer tinkles, somewhere in the no-shit distance, Stringer smiled crookedly and said, "Well, that sure tears it for the two of us. You say the others are waiting on us just a few yards up? I doubt it would count if I foot-raced you the rest of the way. So you just go along and I'll be along directly."

As Dusty Rhodes nodded and started up the rocky trail ahead of him Stringer was sorely tempted, now that the little rascal had his own gun muzzle down to even things a mite. But Stringer just wasn't up to gunning little shits without warning and as things turned out, Rhodes had likely been told as much about him, earlier, for when Stringer called out, "I hope you know I feel it my Christian duty to tell the others you only forced this race to a draw by drawing a gun on me!" Rhodes just laughed back at him like a wolverine leaving a pissed-on trap he'd just sprung, and hurled the cheap pistol down the mountain after Stringer's starting crank, calling out, "Gun? What gun might anyone have drawn on you, MacKail?"

Then he strode on, his back to Stringer as if daring the man he'd slickered to murder him in cold blood, with others within earshot if not in full sight. The now rather pleased with himself driver kept going over the hump until he spied the cog railroad's upper terminal and the massive stone and timber brutality of Summit Lodge just ahead of him. A distant figure seated on the front steps spied Dusty about the same time, so as the driver crossed the tracks he was met by most of the high-rolling sports of Cripple Creek. All of them seemed as surprised to see Dutch Ritter's driver on foot. But Dusty waited until Ritter asked, himself, before answering, modestly, "I did get a few yards higher than that MacKail gent in the Panard, but to tell the truth, the mountain was just too much for the both of us. MacKail should be along directly. We both stalled just down the slope a piece."

Then one of the taller gents there gasped and said, "The hell you say, Dusty. If that ain't MacKail coming at us in that black and tan Panard, I'd like someone here to tell what I'm staring straight at with my own two eyes!"

Nobody could argue, not even the dumbfounded Dusty Rhodes, as Stringer drove across the few flat acres of frost-shattered stone atop Pikes Peak, risked the rope-filled red tires on the gear teeth of the cog railroad, and braked to a stop smack in front of the lodge to call out,

"Howdy, gents. Howdy, Dusty. I see you got here all right, after all. I'd have offered you a ride, had not you scampered like so in the middle of our conversation. Did you think beating me to the top on *foot* was going to cut the mustard, old son?"

The treacherous Rhodes stared at the throbbing hood of the Panard as if he expected snakes to crawl out of it. He tried to meet Stringer's sardonic smile with a brazen grin of his own, looked away, instead, and murmured, "But *how*, damn your eyes?"

Stringer chuckled and said, "You're the one who may need specs, Dusty. For while it's true I needed me a crank to replace the one I, ah, lost, I was able to find another before you were all the way out of sight. But let's not worry the boys up here with such mundane details, now that we've both done our best with results no man here can deny, if he knows what's good for him."

Dusty Rhodes didn't answer, even though he was staring in utter horror at the robin's egg blue crank Stringer had used to start up the black and tan Panard again. Stringer had hoped he'd know what was good for him.

Nobody but possibly a few other sneaks in the crowd could have had any idea what Stringer found so amusing, but he didn't get to savor his own dry humor long. For just as someone was saying something about them all getting on down to sort the bets out with Bert Carlton, a member of the M.O.A. who'd just come out of the lodge yelled, "Bert won't be there! He just telly-phoned he's on his way back to Cripple Creek and wants us to follow, loaded for bear and anarchy. Harry Orchard was just spotted in the gold fields again and you all know what *that* can mean!"

CHAPTER TWELVE

It meant all-out war to the M.O.A. and Sovereign State of Colorado, judging from the way both the national guardsmen and suddenly deputized "Company Police" had set up sandbags and barbed wire all over town by the time Stringer had his hired mount safe again in the livery and himself prudently upstairs at the Cripple Creek Palace with a fine view of the main street from his corner window. He'd left the lights off so he could watch with neither the blind nor risky glass between him and the right-now tense but silent center of town. He'd been offered one of those deputy badges on the train coming back. He'd declined the chore of pulling other men's chestnuts from the fire they might have made for themselves, of course, but he'd seen enough of the tin man-killing licenses to be impressed. As a man who'd been around the rougher parts of a still-rough West, he'd long known there were tin badges and then there were tin badges. Almost any small-town bullyboy could wangle himself a mail order badge that *said* he was some sort of lawman. Even Billy The Kid had been deputised as a so-called "Regulator" for a spell. But as had so often been the case, the real law had inquired by just whose damned authority The Kid had started gunning other young louts, once he'd taken to doing it so freely.

The badges Bert Carlton had somehow wrangled for his own big crew of hired guns had the backing of at least the state government behind them, meaning no judge and jury this side of the distant state lines of Colorado were about to convict or even question anyone gunning anyone in defense of the lives and property, repeat *property*, of the powerful M.O.A.!

Stringer was glad he wasn't one of the union friends of little Glynnis tonight, even as he wondered where the sweet little thing might be. A gasoline driven armored REO with a machine gun muzzle sticking out of its water-heater turret rumbled by below, and as Stringer watched them swing concertina wire out of its path to let it get at someone he hoped he didn't know, he decided the less he knew about Glynnis right now, the better it might be for all concerned.

It got dull and quiet again. Too dull and quiet for a healthy young gent who hadn't had supper to just sit there, listening to the rumble of his own guts while nothing else made noise enough to matter. So he put on his hat, strapped on his six-gun, and went downstairs to see if the hotel kitchen was still open after midnight.

It was and, even better, nobody seemed to pay half as much attention to his work duds and side arm this evening. It was easy to see why. Cripple Creek had reverted to its younger ways, before the big fire, now that gents who'd recently taken to boiled shirts had got out their own six-guns and work duds a man could fight in. Stringer was still a mite surprised when one of the gents he'd last seen over on Pikes Peak dressed like a preacher, sat down at his table with him, uninvited and looking like a saddle tramp he'd never been introduced to before. Stringer was about to say he never gave drinking money to bums who packed guns when the cuss handed a fat envelope to him, saying, "Bert Carlton said I was to give this to you. You won that side bet on yourself fair and square, so Bert sends his congratulations. But he hopes you'll understand he ain't able to celebrate with winners or losers, tonight."

Stringer put the money inside his denim jacket for now. Where he'd carry it back to the coast was his own damned business. When the M.O.A. messenger asked if he didn't meant to count it, Stringer shook his head and said, "Not hardly. I've about figured out who can be trusted and who might not, on both sides. I don't suppose there's any way the more decent owners and more sensible union men could get together and work things out before anyone gets hurt, huh?"

The M.O.A. man shrugged and said, "They know where to find us, if they want peace. Come to study on it, they know where to find us if they want war. We ain't like them red rascals, holding secret meeting in cellars or turning on our own kind like mad dogs just to show how tough we think we might be."

Stringer cocked an eyebrow and said, "I did observe something that might have been a secret meeting, down in Colorado Springs the other night. Have I missed any shoot-outs, up this way?"

His informant grinned wolfishly and said, "Let 'em try. We got every rooftop and back alley covered. To tell the truth, that story about Harry Orchard and some of his boys spotted up among the miner's shanties may pan out no more than a story, after all this excitement, for both our boys and the guard have combed the slopes all around for one stinky whiff of the sneaky bastard, to no avail."

Stringer caught a waiter's eye but still had time to observe that Harry Orchard was said to be slippery as an eel if not downright invisible. As the waiter came over, the M.O.A. man across the table insisted, "We'd have caught an *eel*, if one was here in Cripple Creek with evil intent. For it ain't enough just to *hide* from honest men when you're out to be dishonest. You got to slither out from that hidey hole long enough to *do* something! Big Bill Heywood can send an army of anarchists up here for all the good it will do him, as long as they don't *anarch* nothing. We've got every mine shaft and machine guarded like an old maid guards her virtue, whether anyone's after it or not."

Then he saw Stringer was more interested in supper than old maid's virtues and got back to his feet, saying something about setting up trip wires around his own stamping mill.

Stringer ordered elk steak and mashed spuds, since that was cheaper on the menu than cow steak up here in the mountains, and when it came you couldn't tell much difference if you cut it small and chewed hard enough. The cherry pie a la mode was really made with service berries but when he asked how come, he was told few dudes knew what service berries were and, hell, they were *good*, weren't they?

He forgave them once he'd tasted the home-cranked ice cream and coffee strong as one might be served in any cow camp. As he pushed away from the table, the overhead light winked off and then back on. He heard a distant rumble, then things seemed same as ever, but he still hurried back upstairs to his room, concerned about that window he'd left wide open, for while the evening had commenced dry and balmy as it ever got up here in the Rockies in High Summer, the thunder storms the Front Range was famous for could blow in horizontally and suddenly, and wet hotel rugs smelled just awful.

But as he let himself in and strode to the open window, he could see stars winking above the upwind rooftops to the west. He got there in time to spy what all the commotion down below was about. A puffer-billy fire engine, drawn by six white horses, was spewing smoke and raising dust as it tore past the hotel, followed by men and boys afoot or astride and moving with considerable enthusiasm either way. Stringer leaned out to holler down, demanding some explanation for such a stampede at this hour. Hardly anyone down there seemed to notice. But a kid who'd had to stop running with a stitch in his side yelled up, "The durned old W.F.M. *really* done it, now! They just blowed up a dozen poor souls over to Independence with an anarchist infernal machine! They say the whole town's on fire and the anarchists are feeding women and children to the flames, alive or dead!"

He might have offered more such information, but Stringer had already spun away from the window to cover the story right. He ran downstairs and over to the livery, where he saddled and mounted the bay to ride over to the neighboring camp the radical wing of the union had targeted while everyone had braced for an incident in or about Cripple Creek itself.

When he got to the scene of the outrage, it wasn't easy with so many rescuers, would-be rescuers and national guardsmen yelling for revenge blocking the debris-strewn streets of the mining camp. There was little to see by torchlight, but one hell of a hole in the ground where, it was said, the new trolley depot had been standing earlier this evening.

As Stringer slowly put it together with the help of witnesses, military and civilian, somebody who had obviously had it in for the nightshift at the nearby Finlay mine had wired two fifty-pound boxes of dynamite to go off under them as they crowded into the depot after getting off after midnight. The guardsmen had already traced the wire to a nearby abandoned cabin. The killer had simply waited until he had as many nonunion men as possible at his mercy and then shown them no mercy. Twenty-six men were known dead. Perhaps twice that many had been hauled out of the ruins alive, although some weren't expected to make it and others would be maimed for life if they did. Nobody still alive and full of fight in the vicinity of the

Finlay mine expressed any doubt as to who might have done the deed. Bert Carlton had already gathered a posse to ride out after the sons of bitches, so Stringer didn't have to go. He'd found Carlton a decent enough specimen of the rugged individualist, and knew how he himself would feel in the mine owner's place. But he sensed the trial would be short and not-too-sweet, conducted under the rules of Judge Lynch, when they caught up with Harry Orchard. Stringer never doubted it had been Harry Orchard, either, but he'd have had to insist it was wrong to hang a man without a fair trial. So he was just as glad he didn't have to watch the final outcome as he filed the brutal basic facts from the Western Union office back in Cripple Creek. He knew he was scooping all the other big town papers with his almost eye-witness report. But he still felt shitty as he handed page after page over to the male night clerk behind the counter. He knew why the pretty blonde who worked there had telephoned she was feeling poorly. He didn't know if her fellow workers knew about her mining man, so he couldn't even ask if the poor bastard was dead, alive, or maybe crippled for life.

By thc timc hc got back to his hotel, the night was about shot and somewhere an early bird was tweeting. But Cripple Creek was as wide awake as it ever got, with clusters of men and even women standing on every corner, murmuring fretful muttering and casting suspicious looks at Stringer as he passed, but he didn't get into any real trouble until he strode into the dimly-lit and almost deserted lobby of the Palace.

Most of the lights were out because nobody cared what a moose head looked like in the wee small hours. It was mostly empty because most of the other guests were either slugabed upstairs or out on the crowded streets making war talk. But as Stringer crossed the lobby, three figures rose as one from the fern-shaded lobby chairs they'd been waiting in. Stringer wasn't as surprised to see little rat-faced Dusty Rhodes in the company of Dutch Ritter. But he found it odd to see his own backer, T.S. Murdstone, so thick with other thieves, until he thought about it a moment. Murdstone looked worried as well as red-faced as he blurted, "MacKail, I want you to tell these gents whose notion it was to stuff them flat tires with rope and how much trouble you had getting the motor to turn over, earlier today."

Stringer smiled dryly and replied, "It was yesterday afternoon, now that the sun's fixing to pop up any minute. Have you been accused of double-crossing your, ah, business partners, T.S.?"

Murdstone didn't answer. Dutch seemed to think he was speaking for everyone there, including Stringer, when he sort of purred, "You cost me *money* with your cowboy ingenuity, MacKail. There's not much I can do about the bets so many marks placed on you, save to wait for Murdstone, here, to make it good. But Ben Carlton was holding our own little wager for the winner and it's my understanding you picked up your winnings, earlier. So how's about being a good sport and giving me my money back?"

Stringer smiled pleasantly, considering, and replied, "I *am* a good sport, Dutch. When I win money, fair and square, I consider it my own. Didn't your momma let you play marbles for keeps when you were a kid?"

Ritter stared poker-faced at him for a long thoughtful moment, then he said, softly, "Dusty, get me my money." So Dusty attempted to produce yet another nickel-plated whore pistol, but this time Stringer was expecting it. So the lobby wound up filled with gunsmoke and the dangerous little Dusty wound up running for the front entrance with a bullet-shattered forearm clutched to his breast like a baby, as if he thought he was Eliza crossing the ice with all those mean bloodhounds after her.

Dutch Ritter ran after him, yelling not too brightly about not paying good money to watch someone show a yellow streak on him and then Murdstone yelled, "Shoot him, too, MacKail! Don't let him get away!"

Stringer had no intention of doing any such thing, of course, but Dutch Ritter must not have known how sensible other gents could be, even after you'd been surly to them, so he ran after his small henchman, making all sorts of odd noises, as Murdstone repeated, "Don't let him get away! He's mad-dog-mean and you'll never get a better crack at him!"

But Stringer just stood there, reloading, as the clerk showed his bald head above the counter top ahead, bleating at them sort of like a sheep, to be assured, "It's over, amigo. Do you need a desk-gun, free? Seems someone just left a two-dollar pistol on the rug over here."

Then they all heard a woodpecker rattle of gunshots, somewhere outside. Stringer glanced at Murdstone and said, "Sounded like an army machine gun. You come along with me, T.S. It's my duty as a newspaperman to have a look-see and I owe it to my personal self not to turn my back on *you* before you tell me more about the con game you were helping old Dutch run on the sporting crowd of Cripple Creek."

Murdstone explained some of it as the two of them went out to the street and drifted toward the crowd gathering near the corner. Stringer was able to fill in embarrassed gaps in the small town big shot's story, as the main points fell into place. Murdstone was, or had been, a minor mine owner with a big mouth and a gambling habit. Dutch Ritter was a pure professional whose more socially acceptable business holdings in these parts had been won in various games of chance he'd rigged to avoid any chance of the sucker winning. Having cleaned Murdstone out, and then some, Dutch had offered to forget the markers Murdstone simply couldn't pay, and even grubstake him to a new, if modest start, in exchange for help in rigging yet another skin game.

Stringer said, "Let me see if I can guess the rest, you poor simp. You agreed to throw that unusual race up Pikes Peak, yesterday, only the two of you couldn't seem to drum up much interest because few mining men know all that much about the unusual sport and not many men of any breed have ever gotten that rich making even-money bets. When I fixed your engine for you that time, you bragged on me to all the friends you were out to fuck, hoping some might figure your horseless carriage, with my help, might have the edge. Once you had most of the money riding on your motor car and driver, all you had to do for Dutch was throw the race. Only you forgot to tell *me*, so I can see why Dutch was so sore." Then they were close enough to ask a trooper blocking their path with his rifle at port arms what all the fuss up ahead was about. The weekend warrior told him, officiously, "We're supposed to clear the damned streets. You can't go up that side street. Two poor unfortunates just did and the meat wagon will be here directly to carry their mortal remains to the morgue."

Stringer nodded soberly and said, "We heard the machine gun calling on them to halt. My mother told me never to argue with soldiers blue with guns. But before we go would you mind telling us whether we're talking about a short squirt sporting a pearl gray hat and a much bigger boy dressed more like a banker?"

The rifleman nodded and said, "That's close enough. The corporal of the guard says it looks as if the big one was chasing the little one as they whipped around the corner and tried to whip past our armored car, deaf to the gunner's orders to halt. Do you know who they were? The officer of the day might want to talk to you, once he gets here." But Stringer just took Murdstone by the arm and said, "Not hardly. We never associate with such assholes. So we'll be on our way back to our hotel, now."

CHAPTER THIRTEEN

It took Stringer the better part of a week to cover the big emergency in the Cripple Creek gold fields. Only it refused to pan out to be as big a story as Sam Barca kept demanding by wire, from his distant and hence more excited vantage point out on the coast.

Things kept starting out dramatic enough, but while Jack London always ended his news stories with a neat twist, whether he had to make one up or not, Stringer was stuck with his bad habit of calling things as he saw them, and there wasn't that much to see, once the power structure of Colorado, armed with righteous indignation, had the excuse to really crack down.

Both Charles Moyer, as nominal head, and Big Bill Heywood as the executive secretary of the Western Federation of Miners issued statements disavowing the "Depot Massacre" as even the *San Francisco Sun* dubbed the grim events at the Independence trolley depot. All the union heads managed to do was confuse everyone as to who might be the head of the union while papers from coast to coast ran the pathetic family photographs and otherwise dull obits of the strikebreakers blown to Kingdom Come by the mad Harry Orchard.

Nobody on either side doubted for a minute that the blast had been set off by Big Bill's sinister pal, even though the posse had failed to cut his trail, that night or any other. Stringer had to report the theory advanced by the handler of the bloodhounds hired by Bert Carlton to track the killer down, although Stringer failed to see how anyone knew Harry Orchard had soaked his boots in turpentine, or for that matter how they could say for sure it had been Harry Orchard, once they failed to track him anywhere at all.

Sam Barca ran the turpentine notion anyway and later on, a lot later on, after they'd both forgotten all about his dirty work at Independence, Orchard would be picked up far from the Cripple Creek gold fields and convicted of *another* murder, not connected with the labor dispute Stringer had been sent to cover.

For thanks partly to the wild tactics of the union's more radical wing and perhaps at least as much to the simple fact that the miners were getting twice the pay of, say, a law clerk for eight or nine hour shifts, rough as such shifts might be, the W.F.M. had simply shot itself in the foot, and the M.O.A. set out to finish it off before it could recover from its self-inflicted wounds.

Led by the just as tough but lots smarter Bert Carlton, with the state and local governments backing them to the hilt and to hell with the sissy constitution, the M.O.A. stopped just short of mass lynchings. Union halls were wrecked from New Mexico to Montana. Newspapers sympathetic to "Infernal Anarchists" had their type pied, or dumped on the floor and mixed together, as the first warning. Stores unwise enough to extend credit to any "Ingrate" out on strike were looted and torched by mysterious night riders no local sheriff saw fit to go after, if he knew where his bread was buttered.

Martial law was extended to cover every mining

camp anywhere near Cripple Creek. All saloons, dance halls, gambling hells and gun shops were closed down until further notice. As an afterthought, Carlton ordered his fellow miners to shut down their mines as well. With nobody drawing dime-one in wages until the ''Anarchy'' ended, the results were a downright violent lack of sympathy for union organizers in the shanty towns around the mines. Anyone who objected, however mildly, including the surprised sheriff, himself, was simply tossed into the military stockade to ponder the error of their ways on piss and punk, as bread and water was then called by both those who served it and those who had to survive on it. So most saw the error of their ways right off and some were even allowed to go home and sin no more. But a boxcarload of men on the M.O.A.'s serious shit list were given a free ride to the Four Corners desert country to the southwest and there tossed off in the middle of nowhere with the not-too-subtle advice that their health would suffer just awful if they ever came back to Colorado or, hell, applied for a job in a hard-rock mine owned and operated anywhere by real Americans.

Three or four times that many simply fled for their lives before they could be rounded up. With peace restored the mines opened up again and that was that for quite a spell. The power of the W.F.M. had blown away with the dynamite smoke of their ill-advised attempt to terrorize gents who were just as tough, just as stubborn, and a hell of a heap richer.

Whether fully behind the murderous Harry Orchard or not, Big Bill Heywood would go on to organize the just as noisy and apparently aimless ''Wobblies'' I.W.W. or Industrial Workers of the World, with no more luck, after wrecking poor old Charley Moyer's union for now, if not forever.

Meanwhile, Sam Barca kept wiring demands for more detail and then blue penciling such details as Stringer could come up with. There was no fresh news in the simple fact that American working men were more interested in bread and butter issues than political theories.

In the end, even old Sam agreed Stringer had apparently wrung all the juice out of the confusion in Colorado and suggested Stringer either look into what the union might have had to do with all those mysterious electrical events everyone kept blaming on Nikola Tesla or, hell, just pack it in and come on home.

Stringer hadn't even considered Doc Tesla as a suspect in connection with the half-assed emergency up in the gold fields. Those blinking lights the night of that horrendous explosion hadn't struck anyone as mysterious. The dynamite had ripped out a heap of trolley wire, causing a power surge, causing a circuit breaker somewhere along the line to reset the current, he figured. Then, since he wasn't really that sure what he was figuring, Stringer moseyed over to the Cripple Creek Electric Company to see if anyone there might be able to explain it to him.

The young gal customers got to pay in the front office said she hadn't even noticed the lights doing anything in the middle of the night, that night, since she'd been in bed with all her lights turned off. He didn't ask her who she might have been in bed with, so she repaid his courtesy by sending him out back, where one of the electricians might be able to help him.

He found a tall skinny drink of water in greasy coveralls greasing the drive train of a swamping Corliss steam engine in the generator room. The cuss was friendlier than his morose expression had indicated at first. He said that like the ball governor spinning about up there above their heads, the electrical gear this big engine cranked ran on its own. He heard Stringer out on those winking lights and decided, "Close enough. I wasn't on duty that night, but I heard about it from the night shift. Ripping out all that wire had about the same effect on the system as every trolley on the line starting up at once, overloaded. We got off light with no more than some winking and blinking. Threw the electric clocks all over town a minute or more off, of course. But no real harm done.''

Stringer frowned thoughtfully and said, ''The local clocks got knocked really out of shape the day before, though. Could you tell me how come?''

The skinny and greasy electrician started to ask what day they were jawing about. Then he nodded and said, ''Right. That was no accident. We shut this here steam engine down about an hour, around four in the morning, when nobody with a lick of sense needed any juice from the generators, see?''

Stringer nodded but said, ''That's about the time I'd shut down to clean the firebox or whatever, but I reckon I'd tell everyone in town with an electric clock. You boys made it impossible to open the time locked vault at one bank I know of, too.''

The electrician shrugged and told him, defensively, ''We never figured anyone would want to open a bank vault at four in the morning. As for electric clocks, we don't sell 'em, we just sell the juice as runs 'em and, between you and me, I wouldn't have one as a gift. They make no sense at all, as electrical appliances or as clocks.''

Stringer said, ''I've noticed none I see in passing seem to agree with my old fashioned spring-wound pocket watch, or even with one another. Does anyone know why?''

The electrical expert nodded and said, ''Sure. It's just a matter of electrical theory versus electrical fact. There's nothing much to the innards of an electrical clock. Your pocket watch is a heap more complicated. That may be why they invented the fool things. There's nothing in the guts of an electric clock but a little geared-down electric motor. It's set to turn in time with the sixty cycle a.c. current we're supposed to churn out here at this central plant.'' He squirted some oil down a mysterious rat hole of the slowly turning Corliss as he added, with a wry chuckle, "What we're *supposed* to do and what we *can* do ain't always the same. When you're dragging sixty cycles back and forth every second, and you add up all the seconds of a livelong day, it's a wonder to me them electric clocks ever get close to the real time. We do set out cycles with a regular clockwork timer, of course, but with one thing and another, and the fact that every *other* damned device works just as well at say fifty-nine or sixty-one cycles . . ."

"I got it." Stringer cut in, adding, "The angle I'm after is possible skullduggery someone like that union bomber the other night could cause by messing with the current more seriously. Throwing clocks off the correct time sounds more annoying than profitable. They told me at the bank you can't *open* an electrically-timed lock by switching off the juice. So that can't be it."

The Cripple Creek electrician said, "We've heard about the trouble they've been having with the current down at The Springs. Sounds to me like the time they let that mad Russian plug lightning bolts into their system. Can't say I've heard of anyone down yonder getting robbed with lightning, wild or domesticated, though."

Stringer nodded and said, "That's what I mean. I've got it on good authority that old Nikola Tesla's nowhere near Colorado Springs this summer. He's out on Long Island, near New York City, trying to talk to Europe by short wave whatever before Marconi gets really good at it. So tell me something, as one electrician to a cuss who may know more about cows, is there any way some experimental gear Tesla and his assistants might have left out here could sort of go off by itself, messing up the local juice by, well, *accident*?"

The man more used to such matters in Cripple Creek was wise enough to think hard about that before he decided, "Nope. I've no idea what them eastern dudes had plugged in down yonder. But I do know it was two or three summers back and electric appliances just don't work that way. An electric clock, a fan, something more complicated, is either plugged in and switched on or it ain't. As long as it runs right nobody ought to notice, save for the meter reader, maybe. He'd only notice if the whatever was drawing an unusual amount of juice. If your abandoned whatever burnt out or went on the blink some other way, assuming it was plugged in and nobody noticed who, if anyone, was getting the monthly bill, well, it could play hob with the circuit 'til it blew a fuse or started a fire. Damn white trash will put pennies in the fuse boxes. But as for a play-pretty of the mad Russian switching itself on long enough to turn off half the lights in town, and then just switching itself off again, I'd surely love to see the blueprints of *that* modern wonder!"

Stringer agreed there had to be some mysteriously motivated human hand behind such goings on and thanked the older man for confirming his suspicions. But as he headed over to the Western Union to once more wire his feature editor, he was still stuck for any rational motive anyone might have for playing pranks with the electric current of Colorado Springs.

It had to be some prankster, for the few hitches Cripple Creek had experienced with its own juice had been easily explained by a gent not half as used to the new industry, Stringer suspected, as old Sparks Fletcher, the troubleshooter he'd talked it over with on the way out of town. That other electrical expert had said neither he nor anyone else in Colorado Springs had been able to trace the trouble to its source, meaning that whether he or she had a sensible reason or not, the prankster down yonder was *good* at it.

According to Jack London, such pranks had been taking place for some time, now. Good old Vania had been inspired to come all the way out west for her Czar by the mysterious goings on.

Thinking about Vania made him wonder if she'd still be at the Alta Vista, and still half as fond of him, once he got back there. The little blonde behind the Western Union counter looked just as chesty, come to study on her middy-blouse, and pretty chipper, considering recent events, so he asked her how her boy friend at the Finlay Mine had made out that grim night. She looked blank until she remembered, dimpled, and said, "Oh, I just made that up, to keep customers from getting fresh with me. Did I tell *you* that whopper, Mister MacKail?"

He reached for a telegram blank and said with a sigh, "You must have thought I was getting fresh. I'm still glad you didn't lose anyone important to you in that blast. More than two dozen ladies did wind up widows, in the end."

Then he got busy bringing Sam Barca up to date, saying there just wasn't anything more to report from Cripple Creek and that while he'd give Colorado Springs one last shot, not to bank on anything hot unless the Sun meant to run malicious mischief in distant parts. As he was blocking out his message, the blonde fooled with her upswept hair, murmuring, "I must have taken you for just another cowhand when and if I fed you that line about a hard-rock loverboy. Is it true you spend most of your time in San Francisco, where ladies ride in the park all gussied up in English riding habits and everybody dresses for supper, even week nights?"

He handed her his terse message, saying, "Some parts of Frisco are more refined than others. I'd like this sent day-rates, *por favor*."

She nodded and naturally had to read it as she ticked off a nickel a word. Then she sighed and said, "Oh, dear, does this mean you'll be leaving Cripple Creek right off? Before the dance at the Civic Center this weekend, I mean?" To which he could only reply with a sigh of his own, "I reckon it does. Like they say, them as hesitates gets left out, ma'am."

CHAPTER FOURTEEN

Vania Hovich wasn't at the Alta Vista when Stringer showed up that evening, walking stiffly after riding so far so fast, even downhill most of the way. When the room clerk told him Miss Hovich had checked out shortly after receiving a cablegram in a blue envelope, all the way from Vienna Town, for heaven's sake, Stringer gave himself a mental kick in the ass for having ridden that poor bay so cruel. He didn't even want to think about that blonde in the bush he'd passed up for the sure thing he'd thought he was loping on back to.

The room clerk gave him the same key to the same room and added a yellow envelope from Western Union they'd been holding most of the time he'd been gone. It was addressed to him, of course. He took it upstairs with his gladstone before he tossed his hat on the bed and sat down beside it to tear the mysterious message open. He found it mysterious because Sam Barca had kept in touch with him during his stay in Cripple Creek and he couldn't think of anyone else who'd want to wire him in Colorado Springs.

But it was easier to figure once he saw the wire was from Jack London in New York City, of all places. Stringer had to laugh once he got over his first surprise. Old Jack had somehow found out Vania was Austro-Hungarian, not Russian, and likely more interested in stealing secrets for old Franz Josef and the young Kaiser than any fool Czar of all the Russians! London said he'd contacted Tesla after all, out on Long Island where he was supposed to be. He went on to warn Stringer not to tell Vania this, no matter how nice she was to him, because Nikola Tesla didn't think much of the Austrian claims to Croatian territory and expected his wireless telephone, not telegraph, to win the big war he figured Austria was begging for if it didn't keep its damned hands off other folk's property.

Stringer tore up Jack's wire and flushed the results down the commode in his adjoining bath, just in case. Then he took a leak as long as he was in there and washed up a mite, changing to a clean if somewhat rumpled workshirt from his gladstone as he considered how young the night seemed for sleeping, alone, albeit a mite late to go calling on strange ladies, even ones you didn't care to sleep with.

He told himself it could wait until morning. Then he told himself Miss Hotwire Hamilton didn't have to have a telephone listing in the city directory if she didn't want anyone calling her up at home and that, what the hell, if she was getting laid or taking a crap she just didn't have to *answer,* right?

Telephones had been invented about the same time as Stringer, when one studied on it. But like most of his generation he'd grown up without the dubious joy of using one, much, until recently. As he spread the directory on the bed and picked up the Bell set from his bed table, it developed that the lady hired to help him at Colorado Springs Central had as much or more to learn about the way you got the infernal devices hooked up together. She sounded young. He idly wondered if she was pretty as that Western Union gal in Cripple Creek as she fiddled and fussed, and finally asked a more serious female voice at the far end if she felt up to jawing with anyone called Stuart MacKail of the *San Francisco Sun*. The obviously more mature Hotwire Hamilton, if that was her, laughed lightly in a way that made Stringer feel better about her and allowed she'd never know unless she talked to the gent, would she?

So the gal from Central horned out and Stringer got to introduce himself to the lady electrician. He said he was sorry if he'd called her at an inconvenient time, and started to explain his reasons. But she cut in with, "You must be the gent Sparks Fletcher was telling me about the other day. He asked if you'd been by my shop and when I said I didn't know who you were he told me who you were. Is the *San Francisco Sun* really that interested in blown fuses here in Colorado Springs, for heaven's sake?"

He assured her, "They sure are, when not even licensed electricians can explain it and international spies might be involved, ma'am!"

She laughed incredulously and said, "Sparks assured me you didn't seem a drinking man, when I asked him that time. But international spies in Colorado Springs . . . ?"

He agreed it sounded wild to him, too, but added, "They do like to say that if Frisco is the Paris of the west, Colorado Springs can brag on being the London Town, and you did have yourself a real European count out here before you invited furriners like Nikola Tesla to settle, didn't you?"

This time she really let out a hoot before she told him, "If we're talking about Count Louie de Pourtales and his sweet wife, Bertie, I just wired their Broadmoor Dairy to light up their cows without risking any more straw fires. As for poor Nikola Tesla, he's not an international spy, either. A little touched in the head, I fear, but an American citizen, now, and I'm pretty sure a loyal one."

Stringer said, "My point is that you can get out here from most anywhere, these days, and Tesla was fooling about with mighty up-to-date scientific notions, ma'am. It's my understanding you did some work for him whilst he was out here, trying to talk to Mars by short wave rays or whatever?"

She sighed and said, "Whatever indeed. I only did routine wiring for Doctor Tesla. It wasn't easy. I had hardly any grasp on what he was really up to out here. I sometimes wonder if *he* did, either. Just what do you *want* from me, Mister MacKail?"

Stringer said, "I'm not sure. I know less about petting lightning than the rest of you. Ah, might you have any notion how on earth you can get a light bulb to burn when it's not plugged into anything?"

He was braced for her to call him a drunk again. He was pleasantly surprised to hear her reply, "Sure, with an a.c. induction coil. That's pretty basic, even if it did scare the heck out of Thomas Edison the first time he saw it. You see, current moving through any circuit has to set up at least a little magnetism and . . ."

"Hold it, ma'am," he cut in with a weary chuckle, explaining, "What may sound basic to you and Thomas Edison is pure Greek to me. If I could mayhaps *see* some of this induction stuff at work, I might have a better notion what we were talking about."

She didn't hesitate as she replied, "Come on over, then. I live above my shop near Wahsatch and Fountain. Have you got a pencil?"

He said, "I have the directory open to your address, ma'am. Are you sure I won't be a bother, showing up this late?" To which she answered with a sort of wicked chuckle, "I won't know until you get here, will I? Shall we say twenty minutes, then?"

He said he'd try and hung up. Then he got to his feet, put on his hat and considered whether he wanted to wear his gun as well as a dab of bay rum. He decided he'd better wear it. Her quarters were fairly close to the center of town. On the other hand, that poor bastard who'd switched slickers with him that night had been back-shot smack in front of the railroad depot.

He thought about old boys dying in or close to depots as he headed downstairs. He doubted Harry Orchard could be within a hundred miles of here, right now. There was no law of nature saying the same son of a bitch had to get each and every victim near rail transportation in any case unless . . . "Son of a bitch!" he decided as he hit the lobby, "That's how the rascal got out of there without leaving tracks for those bloodhounds! He just hopped aboard a *trolley car*!"

Then he heard someone call his name and forgot about murdering gents near depots, railroad or trolley, for the gal rising from that lobby chair all smiley-faced was the redhead, the *pretty* redhead, who'd been trying to stop that runaway pony cart, up in Cripple Creek, that time.

Stringer doffed his hat as they met 'neath a romantic palm with fake paper fronds. She kept her veiled boater on, of course, and he saw she was gussied up grander than him in a green summer-weight bodiced dress that made her hellfire green eyes shine like emeralds in her cameo-featured face. He said, "You seem to have the advantage on me, Miss . . . ?"

"Kirkpatrick, Fionna Kirkpatrick of Clan Colquhon, Stuart K. MacKail." She replied with a roguish grin, adding, "What might the K. stand for, Kinlochiel, considering where your people flourished in the Glen Mhor?"

He laughed and answered, "*Comair e tha thu*, and I see you've done some homework, *mo cridhe*," which inspired her to flutter her lashes under her veil and reply, "You don't know me that well, yet. But I did want to thank you for saving me and my wee passengers that time and so I felt obliged to ask around Cripple Creek about you. When they told me you were a famous newspaperman, despite that hat, I assumed you'd gone on back to San Francisco. So fancy meeting you again, here in The Springs! I'm only here tonight, bound for Denver and a new teaching position in the morning, and you?"

"I may be heading for Frisco by way of Denver, ma'am. Right now I fear I have to go meet another lady, and old widow gal, on pure business. Ah, you didn't say what your room number here at the Alta Vista might be, in case I get back soon."

She glanced at the out-of-earshot desk as she sighed and told him, "Not hardly. This happens to be my home town, Stuart. But should we meet in the cold gray dawn aboard the seven fifteen for Denver and Cheyenne, well, I might just let you buy me a Coca Cola in Denver, where nobody's as likely to gossip about such innocent pleasures."

He nodded but told her, "I'd sure like to get innocent with you, for I've never met a Fionna I didn't fall in love with. But don't bet the farm on it, *mo cridhe*. If the lead I'm checking out right now doesn't lead anywhere, I'm sure heading out on a fool's errand indeed! You wouldn't like to give me some Denver address I might want to look up, when and if I get out of this fool town, would you?"

She pursed her lips thoughtfully, they sure pursed swell under that veil, and told him, "I don't think so, Stuart. I mean, a sudden impulse is one thing, while premeditation seems so, ah, premeditated."

He said he followed her drift, put his hat back on, and left to see what old Hotwire Hamilton might have to say for her fool self or at least Doc Tesla. Even if she was as impulsive as that frisky Highland lass he'd just struck out with, and even if she was half as pretty, she didn't have any call to feel half as grateful to him, cuss her self-sufficient hide!

CHAPTER FIFTEEN

But once he got there, Stringer forgave the lady electrician for making him pass on yet another lovely lass named Fionna, a habit he'd been trying to break since the love of his pimple-picking days had wed another goddamn Scotchman. For, while the widow Hamilton was somewhat older, somewhat plainer, and inflicted with a damned old Lowland name besides, she had a nice handshake and served swell cake and coffee in her kitchen, upstairs, while they got to know one another better. The willowy but surprisingly firm-fisted blue-eyed brunette didn't seem too interested in knowing him in the Biblical sense, judging from the bib overalls she'd slipped on over a man's wool workshirt. She failed to pick up on a few inside ethnic jests he tried and it soon developed that her real name was Nelly, that her people had been Connecticut Yankee, and that while she'd heard Hamilton was a Scotch name she wasn't all that worried about it. He told her she hadn't missed much, explaining, "I was raised in legends of blood and slaughter in the glens, but since I was growing up in cattle country at the time I still picture the Massacre of Glencoe as a sort of Miwok raid in the chaparral of the coast ranges. My Uncle Donald told me the Sierras we grazed were a mite high for the West Highlands."

She smiled uncertainly and said she couldn't picture Glencoe at all. He knew better than to bore even lowlanders with such tales and said, "You were going to show me how to light Edison bulbs without electricity, right?"

She sighed and said, "Oh, dear. We do seem to be starting from scratch. Of course you need electricity to make anything that runs on electricity work. It's just that *wires* aren't as important as they teach you children in General Science in high school, even this late in the game. Finish your coffee and we'll go downstairs to my workshop."

He did and they did. She left her shop dark, out front, as she switched on the gooseneck over her stout and well-nicked but neatly-kept workbench. He asked if he could roll a smoke. She asked him not to and stared about in the gloom, muttering, "Let's see, now, where could I be keeping that induction coil I made for that damned teacher that time?"

As she hauled a box over to the back wall to get at the bewildering junk stacked on shelves to the pressed tin ceiling, Stringer asked if they might be talking about a redheaded teacher of the female persuasion. Hardwire shook her darker head and replied, "Male, sort of gray and balding as a matter of fact. Said he taught at the high school and wanted to demonstrate induction to his kids. Never came back for it and when I asked at the high school they'd never heard of him. I think he was just out to pick my brains."

He asked what they were talking about as she got down what looked to be a small wheel of fortune until one noticed there were no numbers on the wheel of artificial amber or whatever. She put it on the work bench and plugged it into the bank of outlets running along the back rail of the bench, against the plaster wall. She said, "This isn't what I was after, but it can be fun and we may as well. When I said that other gent was out to pick my brains I meant that, like you, he perhaps had some basic knowledge of the subject but was way over his head when it got to magnetic radiation. Like a fool, I drew up a set of plans to show him what I meant to make for him. He said he wanted a copy for his own files, and they only charge a nickle for each blueprint, so . . ."

"He only wanted to know how you did, ah, whatever you do with one of those, ah, induction coils?" asked Stringer as she flipped a small switch on her amber-wheeled whatever. She said, "I suspect he built one bigger and more powerful by far than what I'd like to show you, if only I could recall where I *put* the blamed thing."

He asked what the thing she'd just switched on was meant to do. She told him to just watch. Then the telephone on the wall near the back door rang, making her jump, as well. She frowned at him and said, "This seems to be my night." Then she answered it and stared at him even more thoughtfully. He heard her say yes a couple of times and then she told him, "It's for *you*, Stuart." To which he replied, firmly, "Impossible. I never told anyone I was coming here tonight."

But he took the receiver from her, anyway, and even tried to find out who'd called and how come. But even as he spoke into the mouthpiece he heard someone hanging up at the far end. So he hung up as well, muttering, "That's odd. You sure they asked for *me*, by *name*, not just the man of the house or whatever?"

She said, "There hasn't been a man of this house for quite a spell. Aside from which they asked for Stringer MacKail, by name. A stringer is some sort of newspaperman, right?"

He nodded and said, "The Massacre of Glencoe would

take less time to explain. You sure have that wheel spinning like anything, now, Hotwire. How come?''

She opened a drawer and took out some metal thimbles, smiling down wistfully as she slipped them on over the fingers of one hand, saying, ''Kids love this. I haven't done it for some time. Learned it working with Doc Tesla out to the dairy farm that time, only his electrostatic generator was way bigger, of course.''

Then she put her bare hand on a sort of silvery ball attached to the stand her wheel spun on, saying, ''These things only spin with a hand crank in high school classes. Watch the voltage we can get with even a small motor whipping things up to some real speed!''

He started to ask another question. Then his jaw simply dropped as every black hair on her head commenced to stand straight up, with tiny blue sparks crackling off the ends, like she was fixing to catch fire. Then it got worse. She raised her hand, as if reaching for the tin ceiling with those thimbles on her finger tips. She couldn't reach that high, of course. She didn't have to, if scaring him was what she had in mind. He gasped, ''Kee-rist! Are you trying to fry your fool self alive?'' as hair-thin but no-shit lighting bolts commenced to crackle louder than popping popcorn off her fingertips to the tin ceiling.

She removed her bare hand from the ball and admitted it tingled a mite as her hair, having come unpinned by her sorcery, floated down around her shoulders. She added, ''The *voltage* was way up there, but I wasn't taking enough *wattage* to harm a flea. Doc Tesla must have built up tolerance to a good tingle, though. He used to put on quite a show at his electric circus up the slope. Scared *me* a time or two and I knew it was basic whiz-bang blown to majestic proportions.''

She'd removed the thimbles and hunkered down to peer under the bench by the time Stringer had digested enough of that to say, ''Hold on. Are you saying Doc Tesla was some sort of confidence man?''

She hauled out a massive object that resembled a length of drain tile wrapped in shiny black silk thread and despite its apparent weight, seemed to have no trouble getting it up atop her work bench beside the electrostatic generator. On closer examination the creation was mounted sideways on a wooden stand with a rheostat knob as well as a double-blade switch to make it do whatever it was supposed to do. The handygal who'd put it together plugged it in, then said, "Watch this," and turned off the gooseneck lamp to plunge them into total darkness. But then he saw a dull orange glow in the darkness, and as it grew bright enough to make out the outline of the lamp she'd just turned out, he nodded but still asked, "Are you doing that with the lamp switched off all the way?" So she reached out to unplug it as well, saying, "No wires up my sleeves, even if I do have this handy-dandy little device plugged in. You can't see it. You can't feel it, but it's giving off magnetic waves, a.c. magnetic waves, sixty one way and sixty the other way, every single second." She moved her rheostat knob further and as the lamp got as bright or even brighter than before, she explained, "I could burn the bulb out, long distance, but they cost too much, so take my word for it."

He grinned and said, "I do. I think I may even know what you're doing, now that I study on how Edison's bulbs work. The magnetic tingle heats the filament up, the same as if the wall current was flowing through, right?"

She nodded and he asked, "What about other electricated devices?" to which she replied, "Have a gander at my other toy, just as close to the coil as the lamp," and when he whistled at the madly spinning wheel of the electrostatic generator, she said simply, "It wouldn't work with a d.c. motor. Since I used an a.c. motor to spin the wheel its little magnets are naturally in phase with the sixty cycle pulses of the induction coil and the rest you should be able to figure out, you well-read thing.''

Stringer laughed and said, ''I'm smart enough now to see we're getting said sixty cycles from the Electric Company's bigger a.c.generator. But tell me this, could you turn that lamp and motor *off* with your magic coil if they were really *plugged in* and switched *on*?''

She sighed and said, ''I wish you hadn't asked that. The answer is no. Poor old Sparks Fletcher and I have wracked our brains and cussed Nikola Tesla's name in vain, trying to figure out what's been going on here in town for the better part of a month. You asked if I thought Tesla was a confidence man. I think it would be fairer to call him a dreamer with a flair for showmanship and a need for backing. As I've told Sparks and other troubleshooters working for the Electric Company, more than once, there just wasn't anything out at the Tesla labs that could make the juice flow so odd as it has of late. The dear man's *dreams* were way beyond me and even the technicians working closer with him. But the equipment we helped him build was little more than lab curiosities writ large. Let me stretch this induction coil three hundred feet and I'll show you some sparks indeed, but as his Colorado backers decided, after getting nothing for their bucks but big blue bangs, there was no practical application for the expensive toys he made us build and wire up for him.''

Stringer asked, ''What about the night he blew out all the lights in Colorado Springs and set fire to the power plant, miles away?'' asked Stringer, only to be told, ''Kid stuff on a grand scale. Self-taught electricians are always blowing fuses and starting fires in the attic by overloading the circuit or inviting a lightning strike with ungrounded wireless masts. Not many can afford to poke steel and copper thirty stories into a sky famous for summer lightning, but he did, and had it plugged into the town's electric grid without the grounding it should have had. Enter thunderbolt and goodbye lots and lots of more mortal wiring. Everything we put together for Doc Tesla was heavy-gauge and the first thing they teach you in Electric Shop Basics is that an overloaded circuit burns out where the wire's thinnest. Then they teach you that real voltage, say, from a lightning bolt or two, can leap small gaps, such as those left by thrown switches and burned out fuses, to heat things hotter than they were ever meant to heat, so . . ."

"Never mind earlier misadventures with big lightning rods that just ain't there, today." He cut in, demanding, "Tell me how you'd switch blocks of downtown Colorado Springs off and on at will, give switched-off lamps and even folk in bed with no clothes on indecent shocks and so on, with or without these Tesla toys you just showed me."

She protested, "Nikola Tesla never invented anything but the first practical a.c. generators and motors, working with Westinghouse before the turn of the century. That was more than enough. Had we stuck with the direct current Edison and other pioneers insisted on, mostly because it was easier to understand, we would be talking toys, or low-powered ceiling fans and such running on the feeble currents of close-up and modest power plants. Tesla made the big breakthrough that'll no doubt mean, mark my words, an all-electric world by the end of this century. But the poor dear just can't rest on his laurels. He's cursed, or blessed, by an imagination that carries him farther than our science has the tools for yet, if it ever can have them. I asked him one time, only to get fussed at, what happens in the end if it turns out nobody lives on Mars, after all?"

He grimaced and said, "H.G. Wells and Percival Lowell will feel just as let down. But never mind Mars or even the Russian Navy. If you can't figure out who's doing it, can you figure out what it would *cost* 'em, and how they might *profit* from it?"

Before she could answer, the back door on her far side crashed open and two men with drawn guns burst in on them as one. The one who snapped, "One move and you're both dead!" was the same jasper in the undertaker suit who'd started up with him and never finished that time in Cripple Creek, outside the telegraph office. The other was less dapperly-dressed but if anything, meaner-looking. The girl was directly in their line of fire in the narrow confines of the workshop. So Stringer sighed and asked, "Who's moving? I'm the one you were sent after, boys. So whatsay we let the little lady run outside and play whilst we settle this more manly?"

The better dresser and talker growled, "It's not for you to set the rules, here, Stringer. First we disarm you and then we decide the next moves. Miss Hotwire, would you be good enough to hand me Mister MacKail's gun before we continue this discussion any further?"

She nodded soberly and turned back to face Stringer. As their eyes met he nodded fatalistically and drew his .38, He shrugged, twirled the gun on its trigger guard to grip it backwards, and held it out to her. But instead of taking it, she shot him a warning look, materialized a pipe wrench from some damned place if not thin air, and turned with her other hand casually resting on the ball of the spinning electrostatic generator as she held the wrench, rather than the gun he'd demanded, out to the gunslick between her and the door. He snarled, "What's this? Are you trying to be *cute*, Stringer?" as he brushed her offer aside with his more serious gun muzzle, or *tried* to.

Stringer was almost as shocked, but nobody else could have felt the way the gunslick must have when all his hair stood on end and blue green Saint Elmo's Fire writhed all about the wrench in Hotwire's hand and the six-gun in his. Then both the girl and his gun were on the floor and Stringer was firing through the space they'd just occupied. He was more worried about the one who still displayed a weapon as well as a startled expression. It was just tough shit about the horror-stricken rascal frozen in place between them and, to be fair, it would later be established that his sidekick had put two rounds in him from behind as Stringer blew them both out the door into Hotwire's back yard. Then he flipped off the induction coil and dropped down beside her in the resulting blackness, hissing, "Roll under your work bench, if you can. Are you all right?"

She hissed back, "Yes, but there's too much shit under there for me to slip my slender form between. What are we whispering about? I think you got both of 'em pretty good!"

CHAPTER SIXTEEN

He had, it developed, once he and Hotwire had allowed the copper badges who responded to the gunshot the dubious honor of shining their swell new flashlights in the back yard. Stringer's old pal, Sergeant Magnuson, arrived with the detective squad about twenty minutes later to verify both rascals were dead, and give Stringer mild hell for failing to leave at least one of them in condition to explain the shoot-out from their end. Even Stringer had to agree the story he and Hotwire told the law left a lot of loose strings dangling, for the girl had never seen either of the sons of bitches before and while Stringer recalled at least one of 'em from Cripple Creek, that conversation hadn't been all that illuminating, either.

Their conversation with Sergeant Magnuson took place back up in her kitchen, where Magnuson had to allow her marble cake was swell, despite his disgust at the rest of the case.

Seated across from the weary-eyed lawman, Stringer tried, "That thicker-set one couldn't have been out to hold my hand up in the gold fields. What if I just got the boys who got that poor innocent wearing my yellow slicker that wetter evening when I first passed through?''

Magnuson shook his head and said, ''We're pretty sure Harry Orchard was one of the killers that time, wherever the rat's run off to by now. You weren't the one they were after that night. Their intended victim knew he was their intended victim. Young Gorman was working with the Pinkerton Agency and knew they'd found out. As we put it together, he stole your slicker in that chili joint, hoping to make it to the night train north during the power failure as someone else. It didn't work. Sorry about your raincoat. You never made much sense as a target for those union toughs to begin with, MacKail.''

Stringer nodded and said, ''I was told some of 'em, at least, wanted more newspaper coverage than they'd been getting. As a matter of common sense it would have made more sense for them to back-shoot Bert Carlton or even old General Bell if even Big Bad Bill thought he could win that way. But if nothing I saw or did up around Cripple Creek inspired this latest attack, what *could* have?''

As she sliced more marble cake for the three of them, Hotwire said, ''The problem you came to me with, Stuart. The funny things that have been happening to the wiring here in town. Didn't you say you'd asked about it *before* you rode up to Cripple Creek on other business?''

Stringer started to say that sounded sort of complicated. Then he nodded soberly and said, ''Right. Eliminate that cuss getting shot in my slicker, take me off any black list either the union or mine owners might have made up, and my troubles do seem to have commenced before I really knew much about what was going on up in the gold fields. I did poke my nose into past history and they tell me I met up with at least one agent of a government mighty interested in old Nick

Tesla's wireless experiments, dumb as Hotwire, here, thinks they were. So . . .''

''I never said the poor man was dumb,'' she cut in, adding, ''I said his dreams were too big for the hardware anyone has to work with on this more mortal plane. I try to keep up with the field. I know how to read. Anyone can see Edison and Marconi are just plodders, next to Nikola Tesla, when it comes to inventing electrical wonders in one's *head*. Meanwhile, even though Tesla and his backers keep accusing poor Marconi of stealing his grand notions, Marconi's built wireless telegraphs that *work* while Tesla's labs have yet to turn out anything good for more than scaring the neighbors. It's one thing to *predict* sending music, voices and even pictures by radio waves instead of just dots and dashes. *Doing* so is another chore entirely.''

Stringer objected, ''It might not really matter whether something Tesla left out this way really works or not, as long as someone rich enough to hire guns *thinks* it does, right?''

Sergeant Magnuson suppressed a yawn and said, ''This is all mighty interesting, I'm sure, but, no offense, we're now using our imaginations more than any really practical solutions or even suggestions I'd be willing to offer my superiors. So, I'll tell you what we're going to do. By *me* I mean my outfit. We're going to backtrack those two dead cusses you were kind enough to deposit in this little lady's yard for us. After we find out just who they was and where they came from we'll doubtless find it easier to connect 'em up to whomsoever sent them after you, Mister MacKail. That they were after you and not Miss Hotwire, here, seems self-evident. They called first to make sure you were here before they come calling with their guns out. So your intimation that they feared you'd write an exposé about the dumb way this town's been wired commences to go mushy as soon as you study on that.''

Stringer didn't have an answer, so he just washed

down some cake with some coffee and didn't offer any. Hotwire said, "Oh, I see. Anyone fooling with the juice would be more worried about me, Sparks Fletcher, or some other regular electrician catching them at it."

Magnuson nodded and said, "That's about the size of her. Meanwhile the coroner may want a word with both you young folk in the next few days. So can I tell the chief neither one of you are fixing to leave town in the near future?"

Stringer nodded and said, "You can reach me by telephone at the Alta Vista."

"Or here," their attractive hostess chimed in, meeting Stringer's suddenly thoughtful amber eyes with her not-that-innocent baby blues. So even though Sergeant Magnuson only stayed for one more cup of coffee before excusing himself for the night, Stringer could hardly wait for the thick-witted lawman to get the hell out of there and, from the way Hotwire Hamilton responded to his first enthusiastic grab, she'd been mighty anxious as well.

CHAPTER SEVENTEEN

She asked him to call her Nell, after they'd tingled down and dirty betwixt the clean sheets in her front bedroom in a manner that made him suspect she'd wired her springy bedstead for shock value. But as he assured her when she complimented him on his virility the third or fourth time they started over, he didn't need his hair raised by anyone who could raise a man's love muscles so grand, just by looking so grand with her work shirt and bib overalls out of the damned way.

Aside from being soft and satin-fleshed over the shapely muscles she'd developed getting into all sorts of other curious positions under houses or up atop utility poles, the lusty young widow made love in neither a coy nor a sluttish way, as if they were old pals who'd done it before, enjoyed it a heap, and ought to do it some more. So they did it some more until, as they were going at it dog style with the window shades up but the bedroom lights out, of course, the damned lights flashed on, exposing them to public ridicule if anyone was still up just across the street. So as she flattened out, blushing red with all four cheeks, Stringer dashed to the wall switch, flipped it in vain, and had no choice but to charge right at the window, bare as he might be, and yank down the shade as, behind him, the red-faced gal insisted that what had just transpired was impossible.

Somebody seemed to agree with them. The lights went out again. Stringer rose, tried the switch some more, and grunted, "No dice. No juice, either way, now. We'd still best leave the shade down. I don't want to go through *that* again."

She said she didn't, either, and when he tried to take her naked body in his bare arms again she protested, "Hold the thought, darling. Don't you think we ought to search for burglars, or maybe elves, down below? I just told you there's no way to do what someone just did. I meant not from any distance. They obviously just *did* it."

He drew his S&W from the gun rig he'd draped over the bedpost and told her he'd see to it, adding, "What am I looking for?"

She rose to follow, naked as she might be, saying, "You saw the induction coil I made. If they're not right downstairs they can't be far, big as they may have built their own."

As they padded barefoot down the back stairs, he asked what the maximum range of a really awesome creation like that might be. She whispered, "I don't know. I don't think anyone else does, either. I know Nikola Tesla liked to impress visitors by stepping out of the lab to greet them in the open, take a forty watt Westinghouse bulb from his frock coat, and have it light up in his bare hand. The induction coil his assistant, Czito, switched on inside was beaming a good hundred and fifty, mayhaps two hundred feet, but it was really a big one, draining an awful lot of the free juice they extended him until they found out what

Nikola Tesla meant when he said he needed just enough to run a few experiments."

They got to the bottom. He made her stay put as he quickly made sure there was nobody, with or without any mystery gear, in either her workshop or out front. As he rejoined her in the hallway he told her, "Two hundred feet is about the width of a city block. How do we go about getting copies of your neighbors' electric bills, let's say all of 'em at this end of the block and, come to study on it, right across the street?"

She started to ask why. Then she said, "My, you sure think fast on your sweet bare feet. I'm sure Sparks Fletcher could get carbon copies or just copy down those bills, and of course anyone playing pranks like that last one would wind up with one electric bill indeed!"

"For more than one month," he began, then frowned and said, "Hold it. Didn't you say all this funny stuff started about a month ago? Before or after billing time, Nelly?"

She said, "I'm not sure. Let's see, today was the last working day of June. Sparks would know better than me whether the billing for the past month has gone out already or waiting to be mailed next Monday. But . . . *why*, darling?"

He recalled an extension telephone set in her bedroom, so he suggested they get up there, quickly. She naturally knew Fletcher's home phone number, having worked with the company trouble shooter so often. The Bell system, having its own source of the low amperage direct current telephones required, hadn't been effected by the latest power failure. They found out the whole downtown of Colorado Springs had gone dark, again, when Fletcher's wife told Nelly her husband had just been called down to the power house to do something about it, adding, "Thank the Lord tomorrow is the Sabbath!" to which Nelly replied, "Amen!" and hung up. As she lay back down beside Stringer she said, "Dear old Martha Fletcher has a point. With all the banks and most of the businesses shut down for the day, Sparks and his crew will have until Monday to get the juice flowing again and, speaking of flowing juices . . ."

He laughed and took her up on that, but since by now they'd gotten to that pleasant stage where a couple feels comfortable gabbing and grabbing at the same time, he felt free to ask, "Didn't you tell me before, that so far neither you nor any other electrician in town has any notion what's been going on, let alone just how to fix it?"

She moved her hips teasingly but remained calm, above the waist, as she replied, with less interest, "It has to be deliberate mischief. But so far the power's never been off more than a few hours and you just suggested a swell way to catch the culprit, dear. I'm surprised none of us thought about comparing past and recent electric bills. I know mine are much higher than any of my neighbors, unless some of my neighbors have gotten awfully sneaky, and I can't be using the juice it would take to run all that . . . Hold it, run *what*? I just can't figure it, honey. I mean I know how to switch off someone's current from outside. I know how to make their dead house current wink on and off with wireless induction. But I'll be wired d.c. if I can see how anyone could do so without it showing up somewhere for the meter readers and, like Sergeant Magnuson said, there's no sensible reason I can come up with to *play* such pranks, even if I *could!*"

He said, "There has to be, despite how casually everyone in town seems to take the bugs in their electrical system. Call me an old fussbudget, but if I had my life savings tied up in a business or bank amid such uncertain surroundings, I'd be anxious as hell."

She started moving faster, sort of panting, "Maybe you're right. Maybe we've just grown used to having crazy electric current with no harm done. But do we have to worry about it *now*, Lover?"

They didn't, of course. But after they'd finished and Stringer was building a smoke for them to share whilst they recovered their strength the telephone set beside them rang. Stringer had trouble following just one side of the conversation, so he didn't try, and had the Bull Durham going by the time she hung up and said, "That's odd. It was Pete Collins, from the power plant. He says there's nothing wrong with either their new steam turbines or their Westinghouse generators. The current's going out. Folks all over town are telephoning in to ask where theirs is. Pete asked if I had any juice and if not, whether I knew where Sparks might be."

Stringer blew a thoughtful smoke ring and asked, "Where *should* he be on a night like this?" To which she replied, "Out reading meters and climbing poles, of course. I wish I knew where he was for sure, for I'd like to join him, in a more sisterly way, I mean. I like your suggestion about looking through the company records instead of alley transformers."

He said, "I've got another suggestion. Get that Collins gent at the main plant on the telephone again and let me talk to him about those electric bills some more, will you?"

Stringer wasn't as surprised as the rest of the town when the juice was still shut off, however it had been shut off, well after sunrise. He took it more seriously than some, however. Few folk minded going to church on a bright Sunday morn, whether there were Edison bulbs or candles lit up to compete with the sunlight streaming in through the stained glass. The downtown shops were mostly shuttered for the Sabbath. The banks wouldn't open before Monday for Teddy Roosevelt in the flesh. So, as Stringer and Sergeant Magnuson lay belly down in the dust below the porch of the locked-up feed store across from the D&RGRR Depot, the local lawman kept grousing, "Damn it, MacKail. The more I study on your proposal, the less sense it makes. I'll allow it unsettled my breakfast when they told us at the Electric Company how much of their cash reserves they kept at First National, and I'll allow your notion made sense at first glance, when they told us the vaults at First National can't be opened until their dumb electricated time locks get some juice to run on. But as I lay here adding your figures up, they don't add up. You say the electric bills go out tomorrow. I get mine around the third or fourth of the month but I'll take your word for it."

Stringer said, "You weren't listening when we asked them at their billing office whether anyone recalled making out a bill for a hundred dollars or more, as Hotwire Hamilton suggested."

Magnuson shook his square head and replied, "I was listening. If my wife and kids ever run up a bill for more than ten bucks I'd recall it well at my murder trial. They said nobody reading meters or typing up bills has reported anything half as unusual, so you struck out with that angle, too, and how many times do I have to tell you nobody steals money *before* the customers can mail it in, even if they can get into the vault, which nobody, not even the bank president, can even think about right now!"

Stringer nodded grimly and said, "I told you before the name of the game is *complacency*. The mastermind behind all this razzle dazzle is counting on anyone who suspects anything at all putting things together exactly the way you just did. Hold on, I think that's our boy now, I wasn't banking on him having any backing, after what happened to his other boys last night."

As they both stared from ground level at the three men striding toward the depot across the street, the lawman frowned thoughtfully and said, "We'd best do it my way. It's too big a boo, your way, with old Sparks Fletcher guarded by such hulks!"

But Stringer insisted, "It's got to be my way. We

only get one chance and if he's been as smart about the money, it still may not hold up in court!''

So a few minutes later, as wiry old Sparks Fletcher and his much younger and way bigger henchmen stood on the rear platform, anxious as well as early for the morning southbound, the older gent's morning was just about ruined as he saw Stringer approaching from the end of the platform, covered with dust all down the front of his blue denims and letting his gun hand ride casually on the grips of his six-gun.

The troubleshooter for the electric company pasted an innocent smile on to say, ''Howdy, MacKail. You headed for Santa Fe this fine Sabbath morning, too? Meet Bill and Jimmy, my two fine nephews. This here's that newspaperman I told you about, boys.''

They both smiled at him, about as sincerely as a fox smiles at a plump pullet. He didn't want to shake with his gunhand, so he left it right where it was as he said, ''I want in, Sparks. I reckon we all know what I'm talking about and I hope you've seen the error of your ways in sending those other pet apes after me last night. So let's keep it neighborly, this time.''

The old man smiled so innocently that Stringer would have been tempted to let him off if he'd been on the jury, and inquired in a sincerely puzzled voice, ''What are you talking about, old son? You got no possible quarrel with me and mine. It's our day off and we're just headed down to Santa Fe to visit kin. Is there anything wrong with that?''

Stringer smiled back, not half as nice, and said, ''Bullshit. You're on your way to Mexico and where have you hidden the dinero, a money belt or more? I was afraid you'd be smart enough to ship the loot separate and meet up with it somewhere like Salt Lake or Omaha, where innocent old gringos don't stand out as much. Since you're making the usual run for Old Mexico I figure you've got it *on* you. Nobody with such a guilty conscience would be about to trust the

Mexican Postal Service, even in less troubled times. So, let's see, I reckon an even thousand would take care of my own conscience, Sparks. I'm not greedy. What made *you* so greedy, that gold watch and modest pension waiting for you, not that far down the straight and narrow, Sparks?''

The one called Bill glanced about and spread his bootheels for better balance as he softly growled, ''It's the word of three good old boys against one dead pissant, Boss.'' But Sparks just went on smiling as he purred, ''It's a mite public and I'd like to hear what the pissant has to say, boys.'' So the one called Jimmy edged around to put Stringer at further disadvantage, muttering, ''Have your say, Pissant.''

Stringer ignored the two gun waddies, big as they must have thought they loomed above the wily old goat between them. Nothing much was apt to start without the troublesome troubleshooters say so. Stringer said, ''Hell, Sparks, you surely know what you've been up to your fool *self*, with that electrified gear on your buckboard and extension cord long enough to enter a roping contest with. Do you really want me to spell it out for you?''

Sparks nodded and replied, ''I surely would, MacKail. You must think you have a lot to spell out, if you're asking a thousand dollars not to.''

Stringer shrugged and said, ''Last night, whilst you were out in the darkness of your own creation, playing early Halloween tricks with your wireless whatevers, I took the liberty of going over some of the ledgers at your billing office. I figured anyone experimenting all that much with their own house current had to have run up a whopping meter reading. Doc Tesla did that time. In the end, your company had to pull the plug on him, remember?''

The old-timer's smile grew even broader as he replied, ''I do indeed. The asshole was drawing more current than the Broadmoor Hotel and trolley line together, with nothing to show for it but showers of sparks. What about it?''

Stringer said, ''Hotwire thinks he was trying to build a wireless set that could reach Paris in time for their big world's fair. But you're right. I'd have made him pay or pulled his plug if I'd been working for the electric company. His tinkering must have spun the meters like little tops.''

Stringer reached for the makings with his left hand, leaving his gun hand where it was, for now, as he continued, ''The winking and blinking that's been going on lately never showed on any customer's electric meter. Once I saw that, I realized the genius we had to be dealing with this summer *wasn't paying* for his juice. I tried to be fair. I considered some crook tapping into some innocent soul's house current. Both Hotwire and your own Pete Collins assured me there'd still be something showing on some damned meter, somewhere, unless, of course, some slicker tapped into one of those ashcan transformers, up an alley pole. When I made sure there was just no way to switch *off* any of the power mains without simply throwing a damned emergency switch somewhere betwixt the power plant and where said power was bound . . . Hell, Sparks, who else *but* the troubleshooters entrusted with tracing the outtages *could* have played so fast and loose with the current without getting caught? Anyone else would have, or *should* have been caught right off. The only real mystery was how they could be getting away with it. Only there's no mystery to it, once you study on who, the *only* who, who could have pulled it off!''

The moose called Jimmy murmured, ''Folks will be drifting over here to catch that south-bound, Boss.'' But Sparks just purred, ''Let's not do anything we might not have to, boys. MacKail's got a mighty wild tale, it's true, but who's going to buy it without any sensible motive on our parts for such tomfoolery?''

The one called Bill grinned at Stringer and demanded,

"Yeah, what's our *motive*, Tom Fool?" So Stringer smiled back and replied, "I just asked if the money was being packed in one money belt or more. Money was the motive all along, right, Sparks?"

The older man's smile had grown sort of wan by now. He still managed to sound brassy as he asked, "What money? What are you accusing me of? Skimming some of the money from the confused customer's electric bills?"

Stringer shook his head and said, "You wanted it all. You planned to rob your employers in a series of slick moves. First you and your confederates fucked up the electric current here in El Paso County with slick tricks we needen't go into any more. You got folk to wonder if it was something the innocent Doc Tesla had done. You even tried to make me suspect Hotwire Hamilton, knowing she'd worked for Tesla and know how to play electrified magic tricks. You worried more about me than your own local victims, even licensed electricians, because you had them confiding any suspicions they might have to you, whilst I was an unknown quality with a rep for investigative reporting."

Bill almost moaned, "Boss?" But the old man shook his head and went on staring at Stringer, saying, "You're fishing. You don't have anything you can prove. You haven't said why on earth anyone as smart as you seem to think I am would carry on so wild."

Stringer cocked an eyebrow and replied, "I thought I was doing pretty good. After you had the local electricity all screwed up, you had the bookkeepers in your billing department all screwed up as well. You were too slick to go anywhere near the cash drawers. So they soon got used to you working on their side of the counter, instead of out in the field where you belonged. They needed help, a lot of help, from an old-timer with the company, to figure out the crazy meter readings your own crew, innocent as well as crooked, handed in."

"To what purpose?" Fletcher demanded, adding, "I fail to see how I was supposed to make a dishonest penny outten giving the clerks a hand with the confused billing occasioned by all the odd power surges we've been having this summer."

Stringer said, "Nice try, but let's not shit each other, Sparks. I want my own cut and Jimmy's right about the others who might be coming to board that southbound. If *I* know, *you* must know you wriggled your way into the confidences of the clerks whose jobs involve the cash. It couldn't have taken you long to get the combination to the bank vault across the way. Of course you had to wait until you had to be called in a few times to fix the *time lock* after a few of your pranks. Businessmen here in the big city just won't wait for their money as they might in smaller towns. You and your work crew here, got to be familiar figures all along the money line as well as the power lines. I figured this weekend for your best bet to make your last big move for the same reasons you did, Sparks. The end of June is the end of the fiscal year. The money that's been coming in was supposed to pile up as high as possible this month, in order for the outside auditors to report rosy profits and higher stock prices for the fiscal year, so . . ."

Then Stringer was crabbing to one side and drawing his .38 as he saw he'd miscalculated the older man's patience, and *speed*!

Stringer beat Sparks Fletcher to the draw; it wasn't easy, but even as he blew the wiry old cuss backwards off the platform and threw himself the other way to throw down on Jimmy, he knew there was just no way he was going to hit two widely spaced gunslicks with one shot, and one shot, with luck, was all he was going to manage!

Then, as he jack-knifed Jimmy with a .38 slug just above the belt buckle, Sergeant Magnuson at last broke cover to put a round in one of Bill's ears and out the other. As Stringer rose to full height in the haze of gunsmoke, he muttered, "I was wondering where the fuck you were all this time."

Magnuson dropped off the platform to hunker by the body of Sparks Fletcher, grunting, "The old rogue didn't let much butter melt in his mouth 'til he was ready to make his move, did he?" Then he patted the dead man's waist more thoughtfully and added, "Must have many a peso in this money belt, even if it's singles. I'm sure glad for your sake. For it proves beyond a shadow that you had just cause to throw down on this thieving son of a bitch, even though Pete Collins says that even with the current restored there's just no way of checking the contents of any time-locked bank vaults before banking hours commence Monday morn!"

Stringer didn't answer as Magnuson got back up with the overstuffed money bag offering all the proof anyone would ever need. For both other lawmen and rubberneckers attracted by the dulcet sounds of gunplay were gathering around the three dead bodies in ever-growing numbers and conversation was becoming more a shouting match than a social art by now. So he tried to blend into the crowd and, when that worked, he lit out for his hotel to settle up and pack. He knew it was only a question of time before the authorities warned him or Miss Hotwire begged him not to leave town for a spell.

He just hated protracted goodbyes and figured he could file his story as well from Cheyenne, now that it seemed ended here in Colorado Springs. But there was a message waiting for him at the desk when he showed up. Miss Fionna Kirkpatrick informed him in purple ink on perfumed note paper that she might just go for that Coca Cola after all, if he wanted to look her up at her new address in Denver the next time he passed through. The desk clerk must have misread Stringer's bemused expression. For he asked with concern if anything was wrong, only to be told with a gallant grin, "Nothing I can't handle, thanks just the same."